An Ideal For Living

OTHER REBEL SATORI BOOKS BY MARSHALL MOORE

Novels

The Concrete Sky

Bitter Orange

Story Collections

Black Shapes in a Darkened Room

Love Is a Poisonous Color

A Garden Fed by Lightning

The Infernal Republic

Non-Fiction

I Wouldn't Normally Do This Kind of Thing: A Memoir

Sunset House: Selected Essays

AN IDEAL FOR LIVING

A Novel by

Marshall Moore

REBEL SATORI PRESS
New Orleans & New York

Published in the United States of America by
Rebel Satori Press
www.rebelsatoripress.com

Book design: Sven Davisson

Paperback ISBN: 978-1-60864-381-3

Dedication:

Rubén Alatorre, for making Seattle less inhospitable

and

Simon Yuen, just because.

CHAPTER ONE:
GRACE

Palo Alto. Spying in Sphere City. What pasta sounds like.

Grace White gathered her thoughts, clambered out of her car, and took a deep breath: the Palo Alto breeze smelled like eucalyptus overlaid with the merest whiff of jet fuel from SFO. The sky was a fierce shade of turquoise. Well-tended pots of flowers exploded with color at every corner. How long could she gaze at a pot of shocking pink impatiens before her eyeballs burst in their sockets? Before the intense orange of nasturtiums microwaved her retinas? Palms swayed in the breeze; she stood close enough to one to hear it creak. Fronds rustled. Cell phones warbled. She was going to meet a detective in less than ten minutes. In some smoggy Eastern metropolis like Washington or New York, this would all make sense. Even San Francisco, just an hour (or two, depending on traffic) up the Peninsula, she could picture herself in a coffee shop, wearing a big hat with a floppy brim, half-hiding behind a newspaper, and simmering as she waited for Rich and his hussy to appear. The lifeblood of San Francisco, like that of Las Vegas and New Orleans, may run thick with debauchery, but Palo Alto put her more in mind of palm trees, Prada, and particle accelerators. As a place for covert humping, it was just absurd.

You'd think he wouldn't do it so close to home. You don't shit where you eat. It's just tacky.

1

Grace stayed by her car for a moment, at loose ends with herself. She hadn't come downtown to purchase anything, and had no bags (but plenty of baggage) to stash in the trunk before meeting Mike. Perhaps all she wanted was to maintain a sense of contact with something familiar, to brace herself up for what she was about to see and hear – better to center herself with her Volvo than nothing at all. Her own center would not hold, not for much longer.

Grace wondered if she deserved this. She hadn't discussed it with her mother because she didn't have to. Gloria would say, *That's what you get for letting yourself go. Not even 35 and he's already running out on you. Welcome to womanhood. Get lipo.* Grace knew things weren't so cut-and-dry. Rich had had little affairs here and there. Once or twice, years ago, so had she. Nobody in their right mind had ever called marriage easy. Grace thought it was more like driving through New Jersey: when you come to an ugly stretch on the turnpike, you turn your head and look the other way for a while. With patience, you'll be rewarded with greener vistas soon enough.

Rich had never been so open about his dalliances before, so disinclined to care if she found out. He didn't come home with lipstick on his collar or his cock, and he never reeked of Mïasma or Efflúvium or whatever Calvin Klein's newest migraine in a bottle was called. Rich's attitude shift appalled her more than anything: his coolness, his lack of engagement, the way his face no longer softened when he looked at her. His genuine smiles had been replaced by a tight and straining variant that told her volumes more than she wanted to hear.

I am still an attractive woman. No, omit still. I am an attractive woman, period. Or no period. That's not for another couple of weeks. So I've got junk in my trunk. Maybe there've been too many trips to Ben & Jerry's. Whatever. Big fucking deal. I'm natural. I'm real. I'm not that peroxided slut of a paralegal. And I deserve better than this. Don't I?

2

Enough of that. Grace couldn't tell whether the voice belonged to her mother or herself. She walked reluctantly away from her car, running her hand along the side as if trying to decide among the sedans on a sales lot.

Mike looked inconspicuous in his Stanford t-shirt and jeans: just another brown-haired white guy in grad student drag. An unzipped blue backpack next to his coffee table contained a couple of books, but when she looked closer, she saw a rainbow tangle of wires. She thought about asking him to move to a table nearer the door, where the scorched-coffee smell wouldn't be as overwhelming, but she assumed he must have had his reasons for choosing a spot so near the back. Better reception or something. Invisibility. She had no idea.

"Hi Grace."

"Hi Mike. Do I have time for a soy chai latte, or do..." She trailed off. In spite of her desire to appear collected, calm, and above all this, she looked through the coffee shop window as if the Grim Reaper might be outside, staring back. At twenty minutes 'til noon, a line of people already snaked out the trattoria's front door. Rich and his whore must have arrived early. No doubt they were canoodling in an intimate booth, over calamari and a bottle of Montepulciano.

"They just ordered their appetizers. I've already checked."

Grace hated her vulnerability and the way it defined her life. No matter how much she tried to conceal it with venom and assorted bitchery, it wouldn't go away. Shouldn't she be past this insane dependency on Rich by now? Shouldn't she have reached that point where he could no longer surprise her? Sooner or later, shouldn't she cease to care? *He* obviously had. She blinked several times. A twinge of concern for her mascara distracted her for the microsecond she needed. Fishing in her purse for a hand mirror so she could fix her makeup allowed her to break eye contact with Mike. *Get your shit together, Grace.*

"How?" she asked.

"Detectives move in mysterious ways, their wonders to perform," Mike said.

"I'm not sure you got that quite right, but nice try. So how did you do it?"

"I bribed the hostess and bugged a booth," Mike said.

"You're worth every penny I'm paying you," Grace said.

"Are you going to use the evidence?"

Grace nodded. "When the time is right."

"When you've figured out where his offshore accounts are located?"

"No, they're in Zürich and the Caymans, just like everybody else's," Grace said. "I'm not worried about that. He's not hiding money from me…"

Which almost makes it worse. He just doesn't care. He thinks he can just carry on like this and you won't suspect, or won't notice, or something. "Dumb blonde fat Grace, she used to be pretty and now see what she's become." That's what people are saying, dear. "Her husband's bonking a paralegal with a name like Morgan or Britney, and do you blame him? If I woke up one day with an ass the size of two coach class seats, I'd pay for my husband's condoms."

Grace loathed the unwelcome visitations of her mother's voice at moments like these. Some people had superegos. Grace had Gloria.

"You okay?"

"Not really," Grace said. "I'm trying to be, but I'm not. You know. Fake it 'til you feel it."

Mike nodded. "I know."

Grace tried to pull herself together. The cogs and gears in her mind needed WD-40. She asked the first coherent question that occurred to her: "What kind of appetizers did they order?"

"Mozzarella sticks."

"How phallic," Grace said.

4

Mike shook his head. He needed to shave, Grace noticed. She didn't feel the remotest twinge of attraction to him, but he did have a certain endearing quality – some intangible something. Some men don't look like much at first glance, lack the all-American male swagger, and drive a nondescript domestic sedans with three or four empty plastic Coke bottles in the back seat next to a disintegrating gym bag full of clothes still damp from yesterday's workout. Mike was like that, the kind of man she wouldn't look twice at, except in random lost moments when she felt out of sync with herself and the rest of the world. At times like these, she'd think things like *I bet he eats pussy brilliantly*, shock herself out of her funk, and smile again… for a little while.

"This is never easy," Mike said. "Don't be too hard on yourself. This isn't your fault."

Grace flapped a dismissive hand at him and shook her head. Her eyes stung. "Too much water under the bridge."

"And too many dead fish floating in it. Go order that latte, and I'll set everything up."

*

How many college romances last until old age? *Not nearly enough of them*, Gloria said. *Or maybe far too many, depending on how you look at it.*

Grace felt a twinge of self-conscious idiocy as she waited in line. She stared at the barista's eyebrow piercing and fluorescent pink hair and wondered where the last ten years had gone. She heard the wind howl in the halls of lost time. Nobody at Saint Mary's would have even considered facial piercings, back in her day. (*God, and it wasn't that long ago.*) A discreet tattoo under several layers of clothing, *maybe*. That would have been considered racy and titillating, almost trashy but still respectable in a rebel-

5

lious way. Nowadays people walked around punctured and perforated and decked out in more glitter than a Christmas display in Las Vegas...

"Can I help you with something?"

The barista lisped. Tongue piercing. Grace felt like somebody's dowager aunt.

"Chai," she said.

The barista gave her a complicated stare. The gold stud nailed through the girl's arched left eyebrow punctuated her expression of *What crawled up your ass and died?* The girl was a lesbian, Grace realized. She appreciated being checked out – *At least somebody's looking at my tits* – but was so taken aback that her jaw dropped open. She fumbled in her purse for cash, found a couple of bills, and dropped them on the counter without looking at their denominations.

"Was that as weird as it looked?" Mike asked, when Grace returned to the table.

"Is there anything you don't notice?"

"Not if I can help it. That's why you're paying me the medium-sized bucks."

Mike handed her a gizmo. It looked like an iPod, or perhaps a very small cell phone. He then handed her a wire with a single earbud dangling from one end.

"Does it have a nice beat? Can I dance to it?"

"It's more of a waltz tempo," Mike said. "Not too fast, but predictable. If you plug this in..." (He took it back from her and clicked the thing into place.) "You can hear some of their conversation. The restaurant's pretty loud, so don't expect it to sound like your TV."

Grace listened. "I don't know. The girl sounds like Bette Davis after smoking a crate of cigars."

She strained to hear. Bursts of static pummeled her eardrum. She

6

pressed the earphone close, attempting to make sense of the words she could hear, but the signal kept cutting out in a shower of painful audio confetti.

"This is worse than my cell phone," Grace said.

"Who's your carrier?"

When Grace named her mobile telecommunications provider, Mike chuckled into his glass of water. Bubbles formed, then popped. Grace pictured him as a little boy with a milk mustache.

"Digitally enhanced silence," he said. "You never know whether you're getting that famous crystal-clear sound or whether your call's been dropped."

"I know. Rich says the three letters stand for Perpetually Crappy Service. Oh wait, I hear something – they're talking about briefs," Grace said.

"Sounds risqué."

"They're lawyers," Grace said. "Legal briefs, not those Armani things he pays too much for. I know at heart I'm just a small-town girl from North Carolina, but why on earth would anybody pay that much for something you're going to spend all day farting into?"

Mike shrugged. "Because you can?"

Grace drank chai, licked foam off her upper lip (to hell with her lipstick), and listened. She could hear the woman better than she could hear Rich. Their talk of some case that would involve several attorneys and paralegals traveling to France and Belgium sparked interest in Grace. She hadn't heard about this trip, what a surprise. She heard the names of a few cities: Brussels, Liège, Paris. Sounded like Rich might be going, but not the girl.

"I think she's whining because he's going on a trip to Europe and she isn't," Grace told Mike. "Poor thing, can't get porked by my husband in Paris. Awww. I'm gonna shed a little tear for her pain."

7

"Grace, are you sure you're up for this? We don't have to go. They'll be back for more some other time."

"I'm fine," Grace said. "I'm fine." She repeated the lie to make it feel more like the truth. "I'm fine. Look, let's just get this over with, all right? Wait, their food has arrived. I don't want to listen to them slurping pasta. We'll hear enough of that back at the hotel when he goes down on her. Should we get going?"

"You're paying the bill," Mike said.

Grace had been brought up to trust everyone and no one. Every imaginable permutation of social doublethink had been drilled into her platinum-blonde head from an early age. As a Southern woman she knew that *no* usually means *no* but not always, *yes* means *maybe*, definite affirmatives can only be communicated by gushing something along the lines of *Why yes, I'd love to, that just sounds divine!*, and the lady's right to change her mind trumps all. And when you suspect your husband of putting it where it doesn't belong, you take his denials at face value. With all your heart. Even as you scour his mobile phone bills, his laptop, and the contents of his wallet. Even as you program your detective's number into the speed dial on your own cell phone.

Rich's affair would have been easier to swallow (or spit) if, during one of the rendezvous Grace had on tape, he had confessed his reasons. Something like *I still love her but I'm not attracted to her anymore, now that she's put on so much weight* would have at least put some perspective on his behavior, even as the words sent her into a towering, righteous fury. Grace wanted him to say *Ever since her ass got so big, she doesn't know how to move in bed; she just lies there and expects me to do everything* because on some

8

level she knew it to be the truth. She wanted the perfect incriminating excuse: a statement that would simultaneously explain everything, let him off the hook, hang him out to dry, portion out a large helping of blame (with sprinkles and a cherry on top) to her, and yet be lethal in court if she opted to divorce him, which was, in truth, the last goddamn thing she wanted to do.

"You've got more than enough evidence for divorce," Mike kept telling her.

On the phone this morning, when she'd called him to confirm the time and place of their meeting, doubt had stained his voice. Grace had three manila envelopes thick with incriminating photos, plus logs detailing the times and locations of her husband's hook-ups over the last six months. Receipts for hotel rooms, with corroborating credit card statements. Sublime fodder for any of a dozen trashy talk shows.

"Grace, listen. If you don't do something with all that evidence, Rich could argue that you're implying consent," Mike had argued. "Don't forget he's a lawyer. You've gotta act on this, strike while the iron is hot."

You mean, strike while the dick is hard.

Grace and Mike had squinted and strained through the static of half a dozen tapes of Rich on his romantic interludes, and he had barely spoken a word about her. He and his ho (her name was Natalie but Grace could not stand to say it out loud or even think it any more than necessary) seemed to accept the arrangement as fact, as *fait accompli*. Or perhaps they never felt the need to question it. Attraction blazed between them, so they'd acted on it. What was there to discuss?

You're married?

Yes. She has a ginormous ass and I'm not sure I still love her.

Fuck me now, you stallion!

Only that's not what they said to each other. Rich didn't mention her at all, and the Other Woman didn't ask.

Sometimes Rich spanked his girl. Sometimes he made her play secretary, and when he found errors in her dictation, he would punish her by tying her hands together and peeing on her in the bathtub. One time, from the sound of things, he'd even tried putting it up her ass. From the swearing, the attempt hadn't worked out. That they'd immediately taken a shower afterward filled Grace's head with a million morbid imaginings. Rich had always been just kinky enough... physically perfect on the outside, a strapping blond-haired blue-eyed specimen of American vigor, and inside, much the same way except for this one thing – the crack in his porcelain veneer that a Zen aesthete would label perfection.

"You know what good sex is?" Rich had asked on their second or third date. Grace, still naïve enough to believe that the achievement of penetration and at least one orgasm had to be good sex because what else was there to do?, asked him to tell her. He said, "A little bit stinky and a little bit kinky."

Grace had collapsed into embarrassed giggles.

Rich went on: "It's all about bodies, baby. It's natural. I'm ugly when I fuck, and that's how it's supposed to be."

"You've never been ugly in your life," Grace had said.

Back in the present, Grace spoke up. They were walking out to Mike's car, which Rich wouldn't recognize. Grace had parked the Volvo on a nearby residential street, to avoid any risk of Rich seeing it.

"Rich has never been ugly. He doesn't know what it's like."

"Does he have to?" Mike asked.

Grace sighed at him, exasperated. She'd intended for him to say *You're not ugly*, or offer some other compliment, and he didn't fall for it. She wondered if he was gay. (Her brother Robert would know but she couldn't call him to ask.) Mike kept not following the scripts she gave him. Maybe his propensity for the unexpected was what made him an effective detective.

"I guess not. Some people never do…"

Mike pressed the gizmo closer to his ear.

"They're leaving," he said.

"That was quick," Grace observed. Nausea bloomed in her belly. "My God, they're like a pair of cats in heat. Let's get going, shall we?"

*

The health of a marriage, Grace's mother had once claimed, can be measured by squeaking bedsprings. The noisier the bed frame, the happier the couple. Grace, eleven at the time, had been mortified. She had seen her father naked a few times. Something that big stabbing her *down there*, rhythmically, and it was supposed to feel good? Better than anything else in the world? Her mother often wore an outwardly cheerful but subtly disturbing expression that Grace later in life had relabeled a leer. *Better than anything else in the world, that's right,* her mother confirmed. *There's nothing like it.* And now that Gloria had gone on to her reward – plastic surgery and a three-bedroom condo in a gated beachfront Fort Myers development, with stunning views of the Gulf – Grace didn't feel as inclined to seek her advice. Why bother? She was going to get it anyway, from the depths of her subconscious.

Gloria had embraced widowhood the way troubled teens embrace crystal meth. Grace doubted her father's ashes had had enough time to sink to the bottom after being scattered at sea before her mother commenced an affair with a Cuban bartender in his early forties. Gloria and Juan made several semi-illegal trips to Havana each year, checking out investment opportunities and guzzling mojitos. Her mother was the last person who needed to hear about Rich's adulterous antics. For one thing, she had probably already guessed. She'd say, *Just you wait, honey. It gets much better after the first one's dead.* And that would be the end of the conversation.

*

Grace called Robert, who had no business advising on anyone's love life. He walked around in a state of free-floating misery. They'd always gotten along as kids, more so than they had with Flora Trust, their older sister. In adulthood they clicked like Lego blocks on the body issues thing: he was advancing toward sphericity at an alarming rate, just as the growth rate of Grace's behind was only rivaled by remote Bay Area suburbs like Benicia and Vallejo. One of these days Robert's boobies were going to be bigger than her own, not that she'd dare point this out. He was perpetually mooning over his friend James, a little Latin hottie from law school who'd bonked him once or twice before deciding he liked Robert better with clothes on. At times his yammering about James got old but Grace felt she had no choice but to listen. He'd encouraged her to have affairs but she just wasn't good at them. For a married woman who wanted her husband back, even if she had to blackmail him to achieve it, there was no satisfaction in wiping a stranger's jism off her belly.

The conversation turned around to his hairstyle and glasses. Grace couldn't stomach telling him how she'd spent the afternoon – spying on the straying son of a bitch she'd married. (Grace heard her mother's voice: *And so close to home, too! Grace, you ought to put a leash around his thing, and don't let him out of your sight! Men used to put women in chastity belts and now it's our turn!*) She could handle talking about Robert's miseries because they took her mind off the upscale but vaguely mediocre suburban horror that passed for her life. Her red Volvo. Rich's Land Rover, and the classic Lancia sports car he kept in the garage. The jacarandas in front of their home. The little ants that invaded every winter, during rainy season. The individual elements of her life didn't add up to a very rewarding *Gestalt*.

Your whole life has been one long attempt to be someone you're not, Gloria said. *You want to be Suzy Suburbanite worse than anyone I've ever met. You can't change who you are, Grace. Quit trying, already!*

Hell, maybe that was why Rich was shagging this woman from the office. For the adrenaline. For the novelty. To stir things up.

Grace couldn't follow a word Robert was saying. She sipped from a cup of green tea and grimaced: it tasted like scorched rice. She'd let the bag steep too long. She should pour it out and try again. Robert droned on. Thank God he didn't have one of those overly emphatic faggoty voices – then she'd really have been forced to hang up. He had a good courtroom voice, though; it was one of his better qualities.

"I hate the way I look, Grace. I'm sitting here in my office, looking at this pile of work, and it's hopeless. Why am I even here? Why do I bother coming in? You know who I'm thinking about, and it's fucking not fair."

"The fair is where you eat cotton candy and show off your prize billy goats," Grace said. "We live in the Bay Area, not Mayberry. We lead aesthetically pleasing but hollow lives. Fairness doesn't figure into it. At all."

"So I probably shouldn't tell you I'm having a fat day."

Grace, lounging in her boudoir, surveyed her body in a mirror. She didn't like much of what she saw below her breasts. Above, yes, not bad, nice rack, daring cleavage, peaches and cream, lot of potential, but if her suburban sprawl got much worse, eventually some developer would apply for a permit to build condos on both of her butt cheeks and a light rail line across her crack.

She needed to expunge these thoughts from her head. She also needed to have her *chaise longue* reupholstered, maybe in green velvet. Something opulent. She needed to buy new bedroom furniture, in fact, and possibly give some thought to repainting. She needed a drink. Above all, she needed not to be having this conversation.

"No, you shouldn't, because I'm going to give you tough love," Grace said. "You don't like tough love. You like, *Let's go to Krispy Kreme and drown our sorrows in crullers.* You like, *Let's stay in and be miserable together and eat frozen pizzas and drink three bottles of Merlot.* And when you get what you deserve, you feel even worse."

"That was low, even for you," Robert said.

"I can't listen to it today," Grace said. "I love you, honey, but I just can't. This afternoon my detective and I listened in on one of Rich's lunch dates with his paralegal. I lost it when they started eating pasta because it sounded too much like oral sex. Can you imagine my frame of mind right now?"

"No, but I'll never be able to eat linguine without thinking of cunnilingus, which is to say I'll never be able to eat it again, period." Silence followed. "Maybe I should thank you for eliminating all those carbs from my diet."

"Hate me now, thank me later," Grace said.

"So what do I do?"

"Cut your hair. You're balding. Accept your fate and buzz it off. The color you've dyed it is for middle-aged doctors' wives who play too much tennis," Grace said, reveling in the cruelty of bluntness. She heard Robert suck in his breath and felt moist. Finally, something was going right today. "Get different glasses. Expensive ones that don't look make you look like somebody's dad. Get your nose pierced or something. Blow off the dust. Every time you tell me you haven't gotten laid lately, I want to tell you the blowjobs are in the details."

"But I'm supposed to be the gay guy here," Robert protested.

"Life is cold and hard and lonely sometimes," Grace said.

She hung up on him.

CHAPTER TWO:

ROBERT.

Avoirdupois. Steroids and psychic healers. Cold clear glass.

A black epiphany struck Robert at work: he couldn't breathe when he sat down. He needed yet another pair of trousers an inch larger in the waist. Just six months had passed since the last upgrade. Robert believed he looked like a snake digesting an egg, and his favorite coping mechanism, red wine, only exacerbated the problem. At these moments, too early in the day to start drinking, his sister usually provided the best comfort.

Today she provided cobra venom.

He had it coming, he supposed. When your husband fucks every woman in sight, just because he can (and Grace had no idea the extent of it), you're bound to be irascible at times. On top of that, the upcoming business trip to Europe provided a fresh load of angst. Grace knew Robert would be there. Robert knew Grace wanted him to spy. Grace knew better than to ask Robert to do it. Their relationship, while close, was laden with topics they could never discuss, and overt spying was near (but not at) the top of the list.

Robert decided to push her nastiness out of his head, take her advice, and update his appearance. At lunch, he dashed out to Union Square to buy a pair of trousers he could wear without blacking out. If he was going back to Paris, he deserved to enjoy himself, didn't he? And wouldn't an unimpeded flow of oxygen contribute a lot to the trip? Especially on the flight across the Atlantic? He also visited his barber and left with his hair mown down to the scalp. After that, he darted into an optical shop and purchased new glasses. Considering how many of the partners took long lunches to fuck people they weren't married to, Robert had no compunction about his time away from the office. When he got back, Davies didn't comment on the new frames (stylish red rectangles), and Robert didn't point them out. Let the asshole overlook the obvious in order to dwell on the mundane.

"Buzz cut. Nice. Going for that Folsom look?" asked Steve Davies, one of the firm's founders (and a bloated prick of a contracts lawyer), when Robert returned to the office after lunch. Davies had lived with his partner Bruce, a photographer, for a couple of decades. They vacationed at their flat in Paris several times a year and had sex with everyone but each other.

"Wait 'til you see the piercings," Robert said. "Or on second thought, maybe not."

Robert had no intention of getting his parts pierced, but the idea popped into his head. Why not? What did he have to lose? Self-respect? If the big boss wanted to believe Robert had a Christmas tree ornament hanging off the end of his penis, great. Deck the balls with boughs of holly.

Legalese and jet lag are a lethal mix. On his last trip to the Paris office, Robert had subsisted on strong coffee and sticky, disgusting pastries. In the depths of his fatigue, he hallucinated rainbow colors on sheets of paper that contained nothing but rows of numbers. Livid ink from the yellow highlighter pens seemed to hum under the ultraviolet lights. He kept getting paper cuts.

Robert had moved back to the States from Brussels five years ago this week. He looked back on his return as a dreary downward spiral, with himself as the bob weight at the end of a very long pendulum. Reverse culture shock only explained so much of it. The bigger he got, the more his life felt *on hold*. There were so many things he wanted to do... later, when he was skinny again. Robert wanted to unzip his fat suit to let the thin guy inside stretch out and get some air and get on with the business of living... somewhere other than in San Francisco. The thing was, Grace wanted him nearby. He couldn't decide whether he was her security blanket or her increasingly overstuffed psychological teddy bear.

Mentally bleeding from the phone call to his sister, even if he could breathe now, Robert called James. James worked at a nonprofit organization South of Market, earned almost enough money to get by on in this gilded cage of a city, and seemed much happier than Robert would have thought possible in the legal profession. How could James not be happy, though? He was cute, and more importantly, he could still see his own dick when he looked down in the shower.

"I need a drink. It's already been that sort of day."

"Robert, it's not even ten AM."

"Like I said: it's already been that sort of day. Don't tell me you're doing something after work."

"Okay, I won't tell you I'm doing something after work."

"But that would be a lie, because you're having a drink with me after work."

"Just one?"

"Dozens of them. Gallons. We'll pickle ourselves from the inside out."

"Name the place."

Six PM couldn't come soon enough, so Robert skated out a few minutes early and walked from his Embarcadero office to the W, located enough long blocks away that when he arrived, panting and filmed with a light sheen of sweat, he knew his latest attempts at the gym had accomplished big fat nothing.

James, aw-shucks cute and permanently tan, made Robert want to tweak his cheek or his adorable cleft chin every time they got together. James spent enough time outdoors to keep his Mexican skin crisped to a shade of gold most porn stars would envy. Next to him, Robert felt as handsome as a pumpkin rotting on a porch three weeks after Halloween.

"I already have a glass of wine for you," James said when Robert arrived and took his seat. "At first the waitress didn't want to bring two glasses but I told her not to worry, I'd drink it myself if you didn't show up."

"You're so cute," Robert said. "I just want to pinch your cheeks."

James leaned forward, offering the side of his face.

"No, the lower ones."

James pretended to scowl but couldn't maintain the façade. He didn't do annoyance well. His type couldn't. The natural effervescence always won out.

James had heard about a new plague. A repository of vile biomedical information, not the kind you'd want to hear about while eating sushi or rare beef, nothing amused him so much as an article about cloning failures, replete with lurid pictures of deformed foetuses. An epidemic of some exotic airborne jungle rot in Kinshasa or Yaoundé made his day. Tubercular preschoolers in American slums, flesh-eating bacteria, superbugs in Britain's NHS hospitals, hepatitis Z: if somebody just died of it, James could be trusted to know every suppurating detail. Today it was the antibiotic-resistant staph infection nibbling its way through the gay male communities of Southern California. It was spreading. He'd heard rumors of cases in the Bay Area, Las Vegas, and Sacramento. Wasn't that just fascinating? Weren't imminent doomsday scenarios always *just fascinating*?

"I may need a third glass of wine before we move on to the next venue," Robert said, swallowing his gorge. "Assuming the germs on the stemware don't kill me."

James gave a sweet kindergartner's smile. With the innocence of a little boy frying ants under a magnifying glass, he summarized what he'd read. Robert feigned interest and finished his wine. All the more reason not to bother attempting to get laid: he could spare himself the twin terrors of rejection and penile rot.

"Get us another drink, and let's get a taxi down to the Castro. Dinner's on me," James said.

Robert opened his mouth intending to suggest any neighborhood but that one, but he couldn't force the words out. He could only keep recommending places in the Mission and the Haight and even the bloody Avenues for so long. San Francisco is not a large city.

Why do I subject myself to the Castro? Now there's a question for my shrink, he thought. When he first moved to San Francisco, he marveled at the diversity: men and women of all races, ages, body types, and sexual orientations made the Bay Area their home, and more or less got along. He'd never lived in a city where people truly seemed capable of looking past the surface. Now that he'd been here a while, he decided he still hadn't found such a place. The gay-ghetto pecking order pervaded San Francisco just as it does every other zone of concentrated homosexuality Robert knew of: wealthy older men and beautiful young ones called all the shots, with the former doing their best (and spending untold sums of money) to look like the latter for as long as possible. Robert's view on all this was *Strap on the tusks and I could pass for a walrus.* At first he had enjoyed living there, but as time passed and his belly expanded, he burned out on looking at other men the way Alcatraz prisoners used to look at San Francisco's lights twinkling across the Golden Gate. Hence the move over to the East Bay. Inasmuch as he had free time, he spent it on mundane errands on that side of the bridge, in Oakland and neighboring Berkeley. Renting videos, buying groceries, borrowing library books – at least these things didn't involve the ritual mortification that accompanied life in the City.

Without much waiting, they got a table at a noodle restaurant Robert liked. If there was no escaping the Castro, he might as well enjoy one aspect of the evening.

"Check out the two Chinese guys that just came in," he said to James, who discreetly turned to look.

"How can you tell?"

"Tell what? That they're Chinese and not like Korean or something? I don't know. Chinese just have that Chinese look. Their faces are different. The taller one in the black leather jacket, wouldn't you love to suck his balls until his moans wake the neighbors?"

"I don't think sperm mixes well with styling gel," James said. "I think it forms a cement, and you have to cut out that part of your hair. If there's a patch of my hair missing the next time you see me..."

"It's because you had dim sum? I thought you weren't into Asians," Robert said.

"Any race is fine. To be honest, I've been noticing black guys lately. I didn't know you were so much into Asians, yourself," he said.

"Well, I wasn't until I met Lawrence Zhou, and..."

"That was a year ago and you haven't been laid since," James said. "Unless you've been holding out on me."

Robert did not want to get into this. He actually *had* had sex in the meantime. For pay. Several times, at intervals of two or three months, when his pent-up sexual energy overpowered his guilt, he'd ordered in. A smiling boy with would turn up a couple of hours later to relieve the tension.

"Why don't we order our food now?"

James remained silent for the rest of the meal. Several times, he seemed to be about to say something. Robert didn't push. Some instinct suggested he'd annoyed James somehow, but how, exactly? *What did I say?* Robert couldn't pinpoint what he'd done wrong. He tried dumping his usual conversational landfill into the empty spaces: idiocy at the office, the novel he'd just given up on despite the author's reputation, the new one he'd started. James offered a few desultory remarks about an Australian film that had just opened at the Embarcadero. Did Robert want to see it over the weekend? How about the Pendulum later?

Because James had been *noticing* black men lately, naturally they had to stop by the Pendulum, which was the best place in San Francisco to notice a black guy or be noticed by one. Fine. James got noticed by a handsome doctor named David, spent 20 minutes chatting with him while Robert stood a few steps out of earshot, overwhelmed by the crowd and the noise in the bar, half smiling in all directions but avoiding eye contact. James got a phone number when David the Doctor had to run. Early night. Hernia repair tomorrow morning, couldn't have him nodding off while slicing some guy's belly open, could they? Robert, James, and the surgeon left together, and a moment later David waved goodbye to James from – Robert winced – a new Audi Cabriolet.

"*You always get the good ones.*" James imitated Robert's voice. As a boy in North Carolina, Robert had bristled when anyone imitated his speech, but now, hearing his vestigial drawl as filtered through James's accent – Latino Lite, he called it – it was hard not to laugh at himself. A little. In his own voice, James asked, "Why do I see you crashing on my couch tonight?"

"Because you have a flair for the inevitable. I'm not driving back to Oakland in this state, so why stop now?"

"I don't know. Maybe we should call it a night."

"You never lose your capacity to surprise me."

They rode the streetcar up to James's apartment in Noe Valley. Robert leaned against the window and stared out into the darkness of Dolores Park as the tram ascended.

"I have a question for you," James said. He finished unfolding his sleeper sofa and sat on the mattress.

Robert looked around the room. James hadn't spent much on furniture – he didn't have much to spend – but he had taste. Robert wished he knew how to replicate this air of comfortable funkiness. No matter what he tried, the results looked like he'd bought the contents of his home in a single trip to a Scandiwegian interior store: sort of a cross between an airport departure lounge and an upscale psych hospital. It wasn't that Robert had no taste. He just didn't know what he liked.

He brought himself back to the present tension: "After all this time, you've come to your senses and fallen in love with me."

The look on James's face put a stop to further joking. Robert's feelings had receded but he could still see the emotional scar: it resembled the high-water line left by an outgoing tide.

"There's this guy," James said, looking down.

"Okay," Robert said. He didn't want to hear this at all. "Out with it."

James looked up, startled. Watching him struggle to regurgitate whatever he wanted to say about *this guy*, Robert felt dark waves of pleasure lapping against the shores of his soul. Whatever it was, it was going badly, and that was a good thing.

"It's not what you think. It's not about sex. I'm not dating him. It's not… he's not a regular guy."

"He's irregular? Tell him he needs more fiber in his diet."

"He's a healer," James said. "More like a shaman."

"Oh Christ."

One thing you can't avoid, living in Northern California, is the social detritus from the Sixties. The astronomical cost of living didn't force all the crystal-worshipping druids to pack their rusting Volkswagens and flee the Bay Area. A lot of the hippies whose brains weren't too scorched from all that LSD and patchouli had bought houses in the Haight and settled down. Since then, the region had seen a proliferation of New Age healers, shamanic drumming circles, tantric masseurs, and sacred mind-body integration retreats (which is to say, a group of men with too much body hair go up to the Sierra for a weekend to dance around in the nude, make animal noises, and jerk each other off). Robert thought it was all bullshit but had learned to keep his mouth shut. Most of the time.

"This guy at my gym recommended him," James continued.

"What do you mean?"

"You're going to think I'm fucking nuts."

"Being nuts is usually my role. I'm enjoying the change." Robert started to say more but James glared at him.

"He's… it's like…" James looked at his hands. He looked at the wall. His face turned the color of a bad sunburn. "The guy at the gym had a weight problem."

"Am I about to hear a parable?"

"Shut up, Robert, will you?"

Robert nodded. James looked perfectly miserable… and in his misery, he looked perfect.

"Carlos, the guy from the gym, he's been dieting and everything. He's lost hella weight just from that…"

"Good for him," Robert interrupted. He winced. Too harsh.

James put a SHH finger over his lips, then resumed kneading his hands. "He's lost weight but he developed stretch marks where his belly used to be. He sagged. He told me stopped drinking alcohol completely, not even a glass of wine with dinner, and he cut way down on the carbs. No processed sugar, no fries, no entire bag of potato chips with a couple of beers in the afternoon, nothing."

"That sounds like a fate worse than death," Robert said. "Why not just switch to the Broken Glass Diet and get it over with?"

"Are you going to let me finish this?"

"The room isn't spinning yet, but I think it's going to. Wanna fix me some toast and a pot of coffee?" Robert asked.

James jumped off the bed. Robert followed him to the kitchen.

"Carlos heard about Stefan, the healer, from some other guy at the gym. He wouldn't tell me any more than that. Apparently it's like a secret society. You have to be referred. He has to like you. But if he's willing to work on you, he's fucking amazing."

"He sounds like a televangelist," Robert said. "I'm picturing whole stadiums of fainting Christians in Charlotte, North Carolina."

"Stefan is real. Televangelists aren't. Carlos went to see Stefan and those deflated love handles *went away* after three sessions. Carlos told me Stefan could have done it in one, but too many people would ask questions."

"Why? Who'd notice?"

"It's a gym, and it's in the Castro," James talked as if Robert were the stupidest person in the room. At that moment, he supposed he was. "The locker room's a meat market. If someone's a regular, you get used to what his body looks like, even if you're not interested in him sexually. Over time, you see how people progress. I've been working out there for three years, and some guys have bulked up in that time. A lot. Others look about the same. You just notice."

"Like you notice black guys lately," Robert said.

"Something like that. If you were more of a regular, you'd know what I mean." He looked away, pretending to check the coffee. Robert thought James regretted the jab... as well he should. Robert's weight was not a subject they could safely discuss. "Carlos's skin smoothed out. He's one of those Latinos without any body hair, and he's got that broad-chested Indian build, if you know what I mean. I swear, he's *narrower* now than he

24

used to be. He says it's from all the weight he's lost, but I think his frame's not as big around as it used to be."

"You like him, don't you?"

James shrugged. The toaster ejected two golden slices of bread, and James used tongs to maneuver them onto a plate.

"Margarine or strawberry jam?" he asked.

"Yes."

Robert helped himself to a cup of coffee while James produced the condiments.

"I decided I should see this guy for myself," he said.

"What on earth for? I knew that's where you were going, but you're fine, James. You've got a fantastic body. You don't even have any funny-looking birth marks to get rid of."

"I have that scar on my chest." As a little boy, James had knocked a pot of boiling soup off the stove. He hadn't been wearing a shirt. He got lucky – most of the scalding liquid landed on the floor, but he did get splashed. Robert thought the resulting scar looked like a goldfish, a description that horrified James, who wore his shame like a burlap undershirt. Even now, Robert wondered how much the goldfish had to do with them not dating. He had made the mistake of liking it.

"Fuck the scar on your chest. I look like blue cheese when I take off my clothes. What the fuck do you need a supernatural plastic surgeon for? And why isn't he in Beverly Hills or West Hollywood? LA's bimbos would make him richer than Bill Gates times George Soros." Robert glared at James. "There is nothing wrong with you physically."

"Thank you," James said. His eyes misted over, and he looked down again. After a moment, he finally spat it out: "It's my... you know, my *size*."

"I've seen that too, James. There's nothing wrong with it."

"It's too small. It's too skinny, and it's kind of ugly. Jesus, I don't believe

25

I'm saying this out loud. I've never liked it, okay? It's an aesthetic thing. I'm not a bad-looking guy, I know that, but like…" He looked down. "It's my worst feature, you know? I've got enough foreskin to make a wallet with, and my balls are way too small, and they don't hang right…"

"So what you're saying is, you're quitting the law and becoming a porn star," Robert said.

"Fuck you, Robert."

Robert nodded in the direction of the bedroom. "The bed's in there."

"Can we not talk like this? I'm fucking serious, Robert. I've always been embarrassed by my equipment. I was even kind of weird about it when… you know… back in 2L."

Robert remembered, all right. James couldn't do it with the lights on.

"This guy Stefan can change all that."

"Your embarrassment or your bits?"

"Both. Carlos said it's like he has power over the body, to work flesh like clay. He resculpts you."

"And you believe this?"

"I've seen the results. Carlos's body is *different*, Robert. My eyes don't lie. Look, let's be totally honest, here. I know you've kind of got a weight problem…"

"*Kind of?* I *kind of* have a weight problem? James, have you looked at me recently? Most Soviet-era statues are skinnier than I am. I look like something pigeons shit on in front of the Kremlin."

"I'm trying to be kind, Robert. Yes, you've gotten heavy in the last few years, and I know you're frustrated. But you're also pretty well hung, too, okay? I know we don't talk about that any more, but I'm trying to be honest. This is embarrassing. Please don't make it worse, please?"

Robert nodded.

"It's different for guys who aren't ashamed of their equipment…"

26

Robert couldn't keep listening to this. "And this Stefan person is going to magically give you a big swinging *chorizo?*" he asked. "You'll be the envy of all the guys in the locker room."

"It won't be gross," James said. "I don't want to be a freak of proportion. Just... bigger."

"You believe this. You're seriously going to go through with it."

James nodded. "I told you," he said. "I've seen. Not just Carlos, but others too. A couple of other guys. Carlos told me who they were. Then I could see the change. You know, things I thought were different, but chalked up to not paying close attention before. There's this Asian guy in his late forties or early fifties, and like his body fat has completely gone away. He started working out a year ago and nobody gets that ripped that fast."

"They do if they're on steroids," Robert said.

James shook his head. "Steroids make you bloat. I've seen that too. You swell up and you get zits on your back."

"Remember when gay men used to be delicate little sissies?" Robert asked.

James shook his head again.

"I don't either," Robert said.

"He's sporting a bigger dick, too," James said. "He's kind of a medium-okay-looking guy and he's always been nice to me. So I've kept an eye on him. He never used to parade around the locker room in the nude, but these days he's showing his shit off to anyone who walks in."

"So this guy Stefan is like the Dick Doctor."

"It's happened to these other two guys. They're bigger down there, or they've gone from skinny to ripped in the space of a couple of months. It's unreal. This one white guy named Arnold had a face like a train wreck: eyes bunched really close together, brow ridge like a helmet, no chin, bad teeth..."

27

"That's not very nice, James."

"So it's not nice, but it's the truth. If you dipped the Creature from the Black Lagoon in Clorox, you'd get Arnold. He looks completely different now. He's still the same guy but all his features are less extreme. His eyes are farther apart, his brow doesn't jut out like the bill of a baseball cap, and he's got a chin. He's still no prize but now he doesn't curdle all the milk when he walks into Safeway, either."

"How much does this Stefan guy charge?"

"I don't know yet, but I'm going to meet him tomorrow and find out."

"So you're going to show him your...?"

James nodded. "I've talked to him on the phone already. He told me he negotiates terms individually, in person, once he's seen you."

"So you get naked and let him look at you all over?"

"Yeah. He said he's really thorough. He touches you everywhere to find out what your internal organs are like, what their energies are like, whether they're healthy or not, stuff like that. He can tell just from touching your skin."

"Does he charge extra for a hand job?"

"Fuck you, Robert! You don't believe a word I've told you, do you?"

"I'll believe it when you show me proof," Robert said. He sipped coffee and felt his mind turn to cold clear glass. "You show me the before and after, and I'll believe it."

James looked out the window. House lights sparkled on hillsides. Robert wanted to see his face but James had turned away.

I've stepped in shit this time, he thought. But on an atavistic level he knew he hadn't.

"This is strictly scientific, right?" James said after an excruciating silence.

"Absolutely."

28

"We're never going to do this again," he said.

"Never," Robert agreed.

If he crossed his fingers behind his back, would that make it not a lie? He didn't think this approach would hold up in court, but just the same, he crossed them and followed James into the bedroom.

CHAPTER THREE:

GRACE.

Paris. Gilded surveillance. Name That Expressionist.

No matter how uplifting travel may be, even in first class, the soul-deep drone of jet engines pulps your guts and sets your brain to buzzing inside your skull. No matter how flat the seats fold, no matter how clever the partitions between passengers are, you're still trapped in an immense cylindrical second-run cinema that flies through the air at seven hundred miles an hour. You're still breathing lung-backwash and other people's gas. Grace prepared as best she could: Valium to stay serene, a bottle of Evian to stay hydrated, a portable DVD player to stay entertained, a bottle of multivitamins to stay nourished, and a bottle of goldenseal capsules to stay healthy. On boarding, she washed down a handful of optimism with a swig of Alpine spring water, then accepted a whiskey and 7-Up from the runway-model flight attendant.

It's not a phobia; it's just discomfort. Grace reminded herself of this but it didn't mitigate her fears; it just reframed them. *I have to be cosseted in first because I can afford it and because I won't fit into a coach class seat without a crowbar and a tub of Vaseline.*

Gloria had relented to Grace's request to invade the principal on her trust fund. Grace didn't want Rich to know about this trip. She wanted no record of it on the credit cards. (A girl's got to have a few secrets.) She went so far as to type an e-mail to Mike, inviting him along, but she deleted it before clicking on Send. He'd love the trip, no doubt. How many private detectives could claim whirlwind trips to Paris among their perquisites? Plus, she could use the company, or so she told herself. When she broke things down honestly, she knew better. She was on her own this time.

What's the line between surveillance and stalking? Grace wondered. Robert could explain it to her, if she wanted to know badly enough, which she didn't. If the definition became important, she could always knock on his door in Paris and, when he'd recovered from the shock of seeing her, ask. He'd jabber about precedents and tort law, misdemeanors and felonies, the terrible behavior of the tragically jilted. It probably boiled down to some simple concept like intent, an illegitimate pregnancy, or VD.

Earlier in the year, her girlfriend Mary Rose had come home from a weekend visit to her parents in Tucson to find her condo half-empty, as opposed to half-full. All traces of her husband Kevin gone, Mary Rose had first suspected foul play – burglary, abduction, murder. Order emerged from chaos: Mary Rose realized she'd been dumped. Kevin had been acting more and more withdrawn in the months leading up to his disappearance. She hadn't recognized the steps in the dance couples do when they're about to break up. She thought he'd been more polite lately because he'd been in a better mood. She didn't see his politeness for what it was: floral air spray to mask the carrion smell of their dead relationship.

Look on the bright side, Grace said. *He could have taken everything. Count yourself lucky.*

Mary Rose wailed, *Sure, we'd been having some hard times, but oh my God, Grace, how could he?*

During the first month, Mary Rose produced monsoons of tears. Time heals all wounds, except for the fatal ones, and soon enough her damp histrionics subsided. In need of some other vehicle for gushing, Mary Rose purged her soul by writing reams of execrable poetry: *He never gave me anything/ He took/ He tore my heart out with/ One look. He took. He took.* Worse, Mary Rose tracked down the name and address of Kevin's new girlfriend and parked outside the woman's house all night, watching their silhouettes through the blinds. She'd caress the hood of Kevin's car, choking on nostalgia as the ticking sound of the cooling engine reminded her of happier times, when they had shared a driveway. She left her poems under his wiper blades until his attorney told her to stop. Grace resolved never to be that pathetic, and reminded herself of this when she asked Mary Rose to water the plants and collect the mail.

"Paris," Mary Rose had said, her eyes misting over. "How romantic."

"Paris," Grace now said under her breath. "How pathetic." Were they there yet? No, coach class had just commenced boarding.

The flight attendant – a slender brunette thing whose waistline and pert bosom inspired loathing in Grace's heart – raised an eyebrow at her but, being French, declined to comment. She looked down her perfect narrow nose at Grace and asked if she might like another drink.

"You seem very thirsty," the flight attendant said.

Fucking skinny Mediterranean bitch, Grace thought. *You can live on brie and Bordeaux and not gain a pound.*

"I'd love one."

Grace repeated affirmations, to brace herself up:

I'll be fierce and justified.

I am large; I contain multitudes.

He's sleeping with his paralegal, for fuck's sake.

After nine or ten years on the clogged, almost-fogged-in SFO runway, the plane took off.

*

Travelling depressed Grace. Always had, always would. After a turbulent eternity aloft, the pilot came on and yapped in French before switching to English and announcing their descent into Roissy – Charles de Gaulle Airport. Grace tried not to think about the air she had been breathing on this flight. How many passengers had tuberculosis? The flu? *Nothing like a transatlantic flight to make a girl feel alive,* she thought. *And occasionally give her a bitch of a yeast infection.* Terrible airplane food, even in first class, left her trembling. The alcohol gave her headaches. Sure, she had Evian and pills for everything, but they could only do so much. Fatigue still crept in. Reality darkened. Rich was fucking a slut and now what was Grace supposed to do? Put on a brave face (How did one do that, anyway – was it like a masque? Did it harden, and when you no longer needed artificial fortitude, could you wash it off again? Would it also cleanse and tighten the pores?) and make the best of it?

Grace laughed out loud. The joke of her life had no punch line.

Stop wallowing, for one thing. You're in Paris. Go to Tati and buy cheap panties to wear under an exorbitant dress from Chanel. Or, better still, wear no panties under an exorbitant dress from Chanel. Pick up a studly African somewhere, or maybe an Arab, and spend the weekend riding his big fat dick.

Grace thought, *Shut up, Gloria.*

Grace took a taxi to her hotel on the Place Concorde. The tour-guide sights awed her as they always had: the Eiffel Tower, the spires of Notre Dame, the pounded-sugar architecture of Sacre Coeur perched atop Montmartre, the Arc de Triomphe, the broad boulevards, those lovely yellow limestone buildings. Even the novelty of riding inside a Citroën taxi and not a rattling piece of crap from Detroit brightened her spirits. Grace listened to Malcolm McLaren on her iPod and scoured her soul for traces of joy.

Everybody pees on Paris, watch me now, sang Malcolm.

Joy? Okay, perhaps not. She'd settle for vindication.

"He's toast," Grace said.

"*Excusez-moi?*"

"Nothing," Grace said. "Just talking to myself. I'm sorry." She supposed she should use her rudimentary French but after spending half a day trapped inside a monstrous Airbus vibrator, her social skills had eroded just the tiniest bit.

"*Voila.* Here we are, Madame."

After navigating the disturbing-to-Americans ritual of checking in and arranging for her bags to be sent upstairs, finally she was installed in her suite. Whom to tip? How much? And how did one keep track of the countries in which tipping was and wasn't obligatory? Grace had long since concluded that one didn't, unless one worked for the State Department. She offered tips to everyone who seemed helpful and permitted them to accept or decline. Being American, she had the coarse luxury of presumptive ignorance about local customs. Being tired, she took advantage of her cultural boorishness and tossed euro notes around like confetti. Better to be taken for a vulgar bitch with too much money and no manners than to stiff someone for a tip.

From the minibar, she fixed an overpriced vodka and tonic. How much was that, ten euros? Twenty? And what was the exchange rate, anyway? Maybe she should have arranged this trip with Robert. He always knew things like the exchange rate and how to ride the metro. She couldn't deny the benefit of having a brother who both gay and kind of a geek. No matter. She downed her drink, and followed it with a second in less than twenty minutes. Even though it was only lunchtime here, and every travel book she'd ever read warned against this kind of thing, Grace stretched out on her extravagant bed and let the alcohol, fatigue, and Valium traces wash her away.

*

A million writers have raved about Paris, but it has avoided becoming a geographical cliché like New York and San Francisco. Paris is uniquely itself. The average Jean-Jacques or Jeanne Marie on the street walks around with what Grace interpreted as a subtle smile, just a few watts cooler than the Mona Lisa's. Even when the nation is gripped by crisis, there must be a certain smugness in waking up each morning and still being French. You can eat nine buttery meals a day and smoke cigarettes made of pure tar and look forward to living until you're 100, with your final four decades financed by a fat government pension. You get to bask in not being English, Belgian, or, of all things, American. Why *not* smile all day, just because you can?

According to Robert, the contingent from Dufferin & Smuck should be in Paris by now. The three gay ones were staying at the apartment of Steve Davies, a partner who sounded like a clump of slime mold with a Juris Doctor. Grace wondered how Robert could put up with the man at such close proximity. *Because of his apartment in the Tenth* made no sense. Did owning a vacation home somehow make him unique? Robert tried to explain further: *The tiles and the balcony and the French doors.* So? *It's right around the corner from Key West.* So was Cuba, and who wanted to go there, other than the Canadians? And Gloria? *Key West is the best sauna in Europe.* And here she'd thought it was a little town on a spit of land south of Florida. Grace didn't get it and finally quit asking. She told him to stop talking, and fixed herself another drink. Maybe the flat had a bidet with water pressure like the fountains at the Bellagio in Las Vegas, turning every act of personal hygiene into a self-pleasure extravaganza. There was no way of knowing. In any case, Rich would be staying with four or five heterosexual colleagues at some little *boutique alberge* a couple of blocks above the Champs Elysees.

Just a couple of metro stops away.

Or a short walk, if she was in the mood to exercise off a few of the calories she'd sucked down, upon her arrival.

She wasn't.

Instead, she rang the concierge and asked for a taxi.

"*Oui, Madame.*"

Grace loved Paris. On a certain level, she hated it too, but there was room for that in the expanses of her psyche.

And she didn't need to concern herself too much with the comings and goings of Robert and his gay colleagues. She'd hear all the sordid stories later.

*

How does this make me different from Mary Rose, Grace wondered. She surveyed the ornate lobby of Rich's hotel, decided the adjacent cocktail lounge offered a better view, or at least as good, selected a richly upholstered red chair where she'd be able to see Rich arrive or depart before he saw her, and seated herself. Her father had been an avid hunter. Still would be, if...

Grace shuddered. Better not to dwell on it.

A tuxedoed waiter glided up and asked in English, "Some champagne?"

Do I have AMERICAN tattooed across my forehead, then?

Grace nodded. "And something to eat." Christ, it was almost time for brunch. How long had she *slept?* "What's your favorite thing on the menu? Bring me that. And some coffee. I just got off a plane, and I'm dying."

"Right away, Madame."

I should be shot for this, Grace thought. *Or lipo-sucked until my titties*

36

implode.

A few hours crept by. Grace couldn't focus on her book. It's impossible to read when one is scanning passersby, so she gave up and ordered a cheese plate – lavish French delicacies she didn't know the names of. Weren't French cheeses supposed to smell like fermented crotch sweat? These didn't. Some fruit – apples, pears, tiny grapes. More champagne. Caviar on buttery little toast things. Asparagus drizzled with a tangy sauce. She devoured everything and her arteries screamed like lobsters in a pot.

I have no idea how to be alone.

She wanted to talk to Robert about this right now, and even pulled out her cell phone to call him. Then she remembered they were in Paris. Their phones wouldn't work. The conversation would have to wait.

I just want to see Rich, Grace thought. She looked around the lobby. She didn't see him. Dusk gilded everything. She'd spent all afternoon in this hotel, in this very chair (except for trips to the ladies' room), nibbling. Some alchemy happened: the food, the champagne, the nervous desperation of this not-so-clandestine surveillance, and the jet lag all combined to form this one revelation. She had to see him. She knew she should just present herself to the registration desk as Rich's wife, show her ID, and ask to be shown to his (*"their"*) room. She could do that. And she would. But she wasn't ready yet. She wanted to see him without him knowing. Maybe she'd just have another drink first. For courage.

Her mother's voice again: *You're spying, Grace, and it's beneath you. Why not just admit it? You want to catch him with his bimbo, either that paralegal he's screwing or some piece of French trash as big around as a Gitane, and you want to make him suffer. You want to take him to the cleaners, don't you?*

Grace protested out loud, as if Gloria were sitting across the table: "But I don't!"

"Madame?" asked a passing waiter.

"Nothing," Grace said.

I just want to see him, she thought again. *I have to make it happen before I leave. That's not too much to ask, is it?*

*

A full day of surveillance, wasted. Waiters came and went, bringing more food and drink. She suspected they were talking about her, back in the kitchen: *That bizarre American woman, she's eaten more food today than a horse. You can see where she puts it. We should bring her a trough. What is she doing here, anyway? What if her credit card is declined?* Grace rejoiced in not knowing more French. They could say whatever they wanted about her, and as long as she couldn't understand them, it didn't matter. It didn't exist. She decided to stick her head in Rich's room after all, just to look around. Then she'd call it quits for the day. She simply could not camp out here until he arrived because she simply could not stay awake that long. She was drowning in the quicksand of jet lag and alcoholic excess. One quick look at Rich's room, she promised herself, and she'd cab back to her hotel to collapse.

It didn't take much to convince the hotel staff. Some crocodile tears that weren't entirely false. *I'm supposed to be meeting my husband. He's a lawyer, in meetings. I thought he'd be here by now.* Grace told herself she was above reproach. With the next breath, she told herself she was beneath contempt.

She found Rich's two suitcases, one open on a luggage stand, the other on a dresser. His underwear and T-shirts lay strewn across the unmade bed and floor like body parts after a bombing. He was never this sloppy at home. Grace wondered if he'd just fucked someone amid all this mess. She tossed clothes and linens aside in search of telltale pecker tracks. She surveyed the debris for signs of unfamiliar and unwelcome femininity – a tube of lipstick, a pair of panties, a tampon still cocooned in its paper wrapper. She found none of these things, just souvenirs of her husband. The pillowcases smelled like his shampoo; the garments in his suitcases smelled like their brand of fabric softener. She sat back on the bed, pressed one of the T-shirts to her face, and breathed in: *Rich*. Her throat tightened; her eyes stung.

The words *I deserve this* flitted through the undersurface of her mind like subtitles in this awful French film her life had turned into. She tried to turn them off, but they wouldn't cooperate: *I deserve this I deserve this I deserve this*.

"But I don't," she said out loud. "It's not fair."

Gloria's voice again: *What is fair, honey? You just tell me that, and then we'll both know. I seem to remember something about cotton candy and prize billy goats?*

Grace rushed out of the room and cabbed back to her hotel.

Drunk on fatigue and champagne, and with a sense of loss gnawing her hollow, she tossed and turned on the bed for half an hour before the dam broke. She curled into a fetal ball and sobbed herself to sleep.

*

Jet lag is a harsh mistress, and Grace woke up with a start at 4.00 in the morning feeling even more wretched than when she'd gone to bed. She hadn't brushed her teeth, hadn't taken a shower, hadn't undressed. She wanted her husband or at least a teddy bear. (How old had she been when she got rid of her last teddy bear? What a stupid thing to do. She should buy another one at once. If you can't have your husband back, you should at least have a big cuddly teddy bear. And a good vibrator, as Flora Trust,

39

her harridan of an older sister, would no doubt add.)

"Fuck," Grace muttered.

She squinted up at the black ceiling. Vague rectangles of yellowish light seeped through the crack between the curtains. In the hallway, the elevator door opened and closed. Outside, she heard the two-tone caterwaul of a European siren. She tried to block out the sound with a pillow, but it didn't work.

Grace itched in half a dozen places. A dying planet's atmosphere of metabolized alcohol surrounded her. She could smell herself – boozy morning breath, unwashed pits, sweat from sleeping in her clothes, cigarette smoke adhering to the remains of her hair products. Her stomach hurt. Lying there, she felt an alarming rumble in her gut. She knew she wouldn't get much surveillance done today because she was going to spend a lot of time in the bathroom losing the wrong kind of weight.

"I wish I hadn't left home."

The Gloria-voice tried to speak up again. Grace could tell her phantom mother had something catty to say. She'd agree: Grace should never have left home. What kind of woman flies all the way to Paris to stalk her husband? What kind of woman actually wants to catch her man red-handed – or red-dicked, not to put too fine a point on it – in the act with some French tramp? Gloria would imply that if Grace had wanted a quiet, normal life so badly, then she should never have left North Carolina. She should have married one of her boyfriends from college (pre-Rich) and lived an uncomplicated life in some charming Southern city like Asheville or Savannah. Magnolias in the front yard, iced tea on the porch, and a mess of greens and ham hocks simmering on the stove. So far from the palmy Palo Alto lifestyle she'd ended up with.

Grace wondered, *How did I end up with this as my life?*

At home, she couldn't nap in the afternoon. Naps, while often neces-

40

sary and occasionally decadent, ruined her ability to fall sleep. This was the same thing in reverse: she'd dropped unconscious like a stone down a well once her head hit the pillow, but now a hideous energy coursed through her veins. She tossed. She turned. She couldn't stand this bed, these sheets, the clothes she had slept in, and the reek of her unwashed body. A bath in a vat of strangers' sweat wouldn't have left her smelling any worse.

Other people must love travel opportunities like this, Grace supposed. She hauled herself out of bed and made her careful, hung-over way to the bathroom. Her legs ached from disuse: too much time on the plane, too much time in that chair yesterday afternoon and evening.

I'm like the poster child for deep vein thrombosis, she thought. *It's a fucking miracle I didn't fall over dead when I stepped off the jetway at Charles de Gaulle. If I'd flown in economy class, I probably would have. Knowing Rich, he'd sue the airline, win, and get even richer.*

Later, when she felt more lifelike, she'd need to go for a walk. Much later. After nine cups of coffee and various analgesics. She peed for a long time and found herself half-hypnotized by the pattern of tiles on the floor. Shooting pains lanced her guts as if someone had crimped various points in her intestines shut with heavyweight binding clips.

But I'm in Paris! There are no evil days in Paris. The Fifth Republic put an end to that.

Other people love moments like this. You get to watch the city wake up. Funny-looking foreign street sweepers and delivery trucks that look like toys for the children of giants zoom around; empty taxis cruise the streets looking forlorn; yawning waiters set up tables and chairs at sidewalk cafés. Familiarity among all that foreignness. Grace supposed she could go for a stroll and watch Paris open its eyes. It might not be torture to watch sunrise over the Seine. She could pretend she was in a Seurat painting, or depending on the sort of neighborhood where she ended up, a Toulouse-Lautrec. On the other hand, she felt like she'd lost a wrestling match with a wrecking ball. Sunrises over the Seine are best shared with loved ones, and the loved one in question was out getting a blowjob from some random Monique or Babette.

Grace started crying on the toilet. She flushed it to hide the sound of her own sobs. She had money but what the fuck was she supposed to *do* with herself? Why didn't she have a kid or two already, and some semblance of stability? The toilet bowl beneath her emptied with a wet gurgling roar. She felt worse and cried harder.

Pathetic in Paris, she thought. *I am despicable. I deserve everything that happens to me.*

She lasted two more days, failed to see her husband, then stopped at an Air France ticket office and changed her flight home.

CHAPTER FOUR:

ROBERT

Back from Paris. Psychic liposuction. Better scenery.

Robert had fantasized about taking a hammer to these mirrored sliding doors almost as long as he had lived in this apartment, but now, for the first time, examining his body for changes, he rather appreciated them. He leaned closer to his reflection, raised his eyebrows, and counted the furrows in his brow. Were there fewer of them now? Why had he not counted them before? Did people normally count their wrinkles? He needed a baseline. He needed a *hairline.* Had the receding tide turned? If so, the difference could only be measured in millimeters or individual hairs. Maybe his eyesight had improved enough to tell. When was the last time he'd read fine print without magnification? As for his skin, he hadn't counted his bumps but his complexion *did* seem clearer, and his nose pores looked less like the La Brea Tar Pits today. After one session with Stefan, Robert couldn't spot anything specific. *It'll take time,* Stefan had told him. *You can't rush into this. And the first session is mostly about me getting to know your body... better than you know it yourself.*

Robert thought, *But I don't know myself. Isn't that the point of all this?*

He's a normal-looking guy, James had promised. The word *normal* in the Bay Area is hard to pin down, at best. What's normal in the most culturally diverse urban area in the country? James's interpretation of the term, in this case, turned out to be a blond white guy – handsome in a bland way – with a German accent but no other visible cues to his ethnic origins. He extended a hand to shake, then ushered Robert (late after roaming side streets for 20 minutes, because the best way to find parking in San Francisco is to leave your car in Las Vegas and walk) into the apartment. Robert rang the doorbell, expecting a cross between Gandalf and the Wizard of Oz. Instead, he got someone attractively nondescript. Robert's attention rolled off him like water on wax paper.

He'd make an ideal actor for TV commercials, Robert thought. *I'd buy a Toyota from him.*

But what he said was, "Hi. I'm an admirer of your work?"

"James said he had shown you," Stefan said. "I trust you both enjoyed yourselves."

Robert took a seat on his leather sofa, a well worn-in black thing that looked cold but wasn't, and looked around the room. Stefan's tastes ran in all directions. None of the furniture matched. Pictures hung at varying heights. The coffee table could not be seen beneath heaps of magazines, dirty dishes and glasses, DVDs, and remote controls. The mess appalled Robert but he had to give the man credit: at least the place looked as if someone with an actual personality lived there. This was not the case at his own home.

"He showed me, all right."

"You liked what you saw?"

"Why do I think you already know the answer to that?"

"James told me you had a little crush on him, and showing you the way he did was not a good idea in retrospect," Stefan said. "It's nothing to be ashamed of. He's a handsome man. It was a pleasure to touch him and work on him and make him even more perfect." (Robert guessed that answered *that* question.) "Plus, you came, didn't you?"

"What does that have to do with James?"

"Nothing at all. You're here because of yourself. Robert. I'm guessing you want that belly to go away and maybe your hair back, right?"

"You guessed right."

Stefan asked what else. Then, "Why don't we go into my studio – that's what I call it; it sounds more inviting than *operating room* and less pretentious than *salon* – and you can disrobe. I'll let you show me what you'd like to change."

"Before we do that, I have a couple of questions."

Stefan had half-stood, in anticipation of leaving the room. He sat down again. The bland expression on his face never flickered. *We have all the time in the world,* he seemed to be saying.

"Ask away," he said.

"I want to understand what I'm getting into, before I get myself into it."

"Of course."

"How does it work?"

Stefan rubbed his hands together. "Think of the body as clay. Living tissue responds to certain stimuli, doesn't it? For instance, if you clench the muscles in your neck and shoulders, and that tension settles in and forms a knot, then over time, you'll develop problems with your spine."

"I'm with you so far."

"I am able to manipulate those tissues, reshape them, or remove them altogether. Don't ask me why because I don't know the answer. It's a gift that runs in my family."

"There are more of you?"

Stefan nodded. "I have a sister in Southern California and a brother in Berlin. We all have the same talent."

"So you can reshape bodies and so forth, just by…"

"Putting my hands on them and telling them to move."

"It sounds kind of..."

"I know how it sounds," Stefan said. "Like faith healers on TV. But they're selling fake miracles and I'm selling – although I don't like to call it that – something more tangible. You can see the results. And I'd be lying if I said I didn't enjoy that aspect of my work. James in particular... he didn't really need what I did for him, but now it's done, and he's happier."

Robert thought, *Happier? That's unlikely. He'll just find another place to store his angst. Maybe Stefan has been blowing him for a few months. Kind of an aperitif after the supernatural prostate massage. Ah, the sweet chainsaw of jealousy.*

"In your case, I would ask you to lie on my table, and I would put you to sleep first. The removal of fat is a very different process: subtraction, not addition. I have to ask the body to relinquish a part of itself. It takes persuasion. When the body is ready, I reach through the skin and simply scoop out the fat one handful at a time. Then the excess skin has to shrink down to size. I have to smooth out the belly, the arms, the legs, the buttocks, the neck, sometimes even the face. You aren't as large as some of the people I've helped, but you need to understand it will take time."

"How much time?"

"I could do it all right now but you don't want people to think you're sick," Stefan said. "You need to make a pretense of dieting, going to the gym, or something like that. Eliminate carbohydrates. Go on the grapefruit diet. When you eat business lunches, order nothing but salad and hot tea. Your appetite will decrease after this session, so that part should be easy for you. Or invent a life crisis and pretend you're insane with grief, if you like. It's up to you. I'd say three months is a good estimate, maybe four or five if you want to be conservative."

"And less if I'm in a hurry? I want this shit to come off," Robert said, pinching a roll of the flab at his midsection. "I'm fucking tired of feeling myself jiggle when I climb stairs. If I want jiggles, I'll eat a bowl of Jello."

"Very well then. How about the hair? How does a full head of hair sound?"

"Like a Rogaine commercial."

"I can tell you're impatient to begin."

"What tipped you off?"

"I'm psychic," Stefan said.

*

In the first session, Stefan started by rubbing Robert's scalp with a slow circular motion. His face softened like warm butter. Robert had always been a sucker for massage, especially his head. His eyes closed of their own accord. Knots in his back untied themselves and his buttocks unclenched. Through the twilight fuzziness, he could sometimes look up and out and down ... in and out... in fact, at times it had felt as if Stefan's hands were inside him, breaking the surface of his skin and exploring his guts as if his body were no more substantial than a bowl of gelatin and Stefan were reaching inside to palpate chunks of fruit.

What do internal organs feel like, anyway? Boneless, skinless chicken breasts? Rotten tulip bulbs? Oranges you've dropped on the floor one time too many?

Stefan had rearranged things here and there the way that Robert would rearrange punctuation marks and fix typos while writing a brief. Even before using spell check, he'd make small tweaks to the text. Stefan's first session had ostensibly gone the same way.

And now?

Robert shook his head in the mirror. He touched himself here and there – his skin, the crow's feet at the corners of his eyes, the creases where his belly sagged over his lap – but couldn't put his finger on what had changed, if anything. He couldn't decide whether or not to be disappointed. How much had he expected, going into this?

"But I don't *feel* the same," he insisted.

It was like getting religion, he supposed. You look the same, nothing's quantifiably different, but it's how you *feel*. Exfoliate for Jesus.

Robert picked up the garbage can from its space between the bathroom sink and the toilet. Wincing at the astringent reek wafting into his sinuses, he used a wad of Kleenex to compact the layer of post-hygienic debris in the can. He didn't want to touch used tangles of dental floss and other personal maintenance detritus. Then he dropped pots and jars of age-defying cosmetics into the can. Alpha-hydroxy this. Antioxidant that. Green tea the other goddamn thing. Aloe vera, glory hallelujah. All gone.

Grace was on the phone:

"I went to Paris."

Robert snapped out of his post-Stefan reverie. He couldn't stop touching himself. He hadn't been this fascinated with his body since the hormonal horror show of adolescence. Now as then, guilt infused his fascination. So did horniness. Any minute now he would either have to jerk off or go nuts from sperm poisoning. On some level he appreciated the phone ringing when he did. Nothing like postponing gratification. Abstinence makes the cock shoot farther.

"You did *what?*"

"I went to Paris. That big city in France? You know, where they speak French and have dog doo on the sidewalks?"

"Somebody's on their heavy flow day," Robert said. He thought of James. He wondered if James had friends or relatives he traded insulting endearments with on the phone. Probably not. He'd have mentioned it by now. Slightly-older sisters you can verbally abuse, and who verbally abuse you back, aren't a luxury everyone has. "Wanna call me back after you've dammed it up with a Tampax?"

"Speak for yourself, asshole. At least when I get fucked, the dick touches the sides."

"You're only tight from lack of use, Grace. Do you remember your husband's name? Does he remember yours?"

Grace stayed silent a second longer than usual. Robert wondered if he'd gone too far.

"Am I getting through, Robert? I went to *Paris*? While you were *there*? And I didn't call you *on purpose*? I was there to spy on Rich." Grace sounded like she hadn't slept in a month and the nightmares had spilled over into her waking life. "Now that I'm back, I'm kind of disgusted with myself."

"I don't know, Grace. Going to Paris isn't supposed to cause self-disgust, unless you missed the Musée d'Orsay and neglected to shop."

"I didn't buy a goddamn thing except food and some paracetamol for a headache. When I got there I sucked down one drink after another like one of those lushes on *Ab Fab*."

"You didn't go to Chanel?"

"I didn't go to the *bathroom* unless it was absolutely necessary."

"And even then, you held it until it hurt, just in case Rich walked by while you were on the can."

"How'd you guess?"

"Maybe it has something to do with knowing you. This was because of the company trip, wasn't it? You wanted to catch him with another woman."

Guilt polluted Robert's guts. He remembered bumping into his broth-

49

er-in-law at a brasserie with a beautiful Asian woman. Rich looked up with surprise and embarrassment at war on his face for a telling few seconds until he could muster a more confident look.

"Minh, these are my colleagues Robert and…"

Hands were shaken briskly, smiles exchanged like foreign currency.

Colleague, as opposed to *brother-in-law*. Robert chose not to comment.

I didn't actually catch Rich in flagrante. He's a pussy hound and everyone knows it, including Grace. But without seeing lipstick on his collar or sperm stains on her dress, what can I say?

"Or *not* catch him," Grace said. "I don't know what to think. He barely returned to his hotel room. After camping out in the lobby for three days, I gave up on the whole thing and came home. I was sure I'd catch him with some French vixenette with a waistline as big around as a *batard*, but it's like he wasn't even there."

"Very mysterious," Robert said, hating himself. "I saw him at work but we all went our separate ways afterward. I have no idea what he did with his free time, not that there was much of it."

"But why didn't he come back to his hotel?" Grace wailed.

Robert held the phone away from his ear. What a voice that woman had. She could blast perfectly round holes in panes of glass.

"I don't know," Robert said. He took a deep breath. "Maybe he was up to something after all. You know how men are."

"Are you sure?" Grace asked.

Robert squirmed. He wanted to look at himself in the bathroom mirror again. He wanted to see whether he'd lost weight. Maybe his body hair had thinned or a few of the zits on his ass had evaporated. He kept thinking of new body parts to inspect.

"I'm a man," he said. "And I sleep with them too. If that doesn't make me an expert, what would?"

"So you think Rich was fucking somebody else while I was there. Right under my nose. He was with another woman."

"I didn't hear a question in any of that," Robert said. "Want to try those sentences again and see how they sound with question marks at the end?"

Grace released an exasperated sigh. Robert could picture the scowl on her face. Her delicately plucked eyebrows would form an obtuse angle on her forehead, like a check mark with sides of equal length or a V that has been squashed almost flat. She'd have that end-of-the-day look he'd been seeing for years: pores visible under disintegrating make-up, hair coming undone, clothes rumpled. At these moments, she was at her most endearing.

Even with the extra weight on her frame, Grace had a presence she didn't give herself credit for. Robert could not claim the same appeal. He knew it. Men's gazes ricocheted off him; the only time anyone looked at him for long was to check out his beach ball of a physique. He felt like a round hand mirror, held up by others to assure themselves that they looked good in comparison.

"What am I going to do?" Grace asked the question after another one of those uncharacteristic long silences. Robert had never heard her sound so sad. "I'm going to lose my husband."

The husband I never liked in the first place.

"There's someone I should possibly introduce you to." Robert spoke slowly and cautiously. "I think I know someone who might be able to help."

"I am not going to another goddamn therapist," Grace snapped. "What the hell does *healing around food* mean anyway? Your support group joins hands in a circle around a chocolate cake and chants affirmations at it? And if you think I'm going to join another goddamn weight loss group, you need medication. The people at Jenny Craig and Weight Watchers know me by name, Robert. They know my car. I pull into the parking lot and they say, *Grace is back again* and take bets on what size dress I'll have on when I walk in the door."

The words *psychic liposuction* crossed Robert's mind. Whatever Stefan did, was there a psychological component? Did he put you in some kind of trance, in order to convince you your appetite was gone and you looked great? How many of the changes he supposedly wrought were just power of suggestion?

"No, this guy is nothing like that," Robert said. "A friend referred me. He's like a psychic naturopath or something."

"So he'll burn incense cones on my ass and chant over me before he gives me an herbal enema and I die of anal toxic shock syndrome."

"I'll check him out and get back to you," Robert said. No point telling her that he'd already been. The disappearance of James's foreskin was all it had taken to convince him that Stefan had more to offer than, as Grace put it, affirmations and healing around food.

"You do that." Grace hung up on him.

CHAPTER FIVE:

GRACE

Affirmations and reclamations. Mimosas. Wiccans with mirrors.

RECLAIM YOUR PERSONAL POWER!
RECLAIM YOUR RELATIONSHIP!
A Workshop For All Women
Nananne Dykstra–Worthington, MSW, and Belinda Wolfwomon, BA/CI/
CT, lead you on a journey of fulfillment and empowerment, out of the darkest
corners of your womansoul, out of spiritual impoverishment and other-centered
choices, into the clear white light of true self-actualization and enhanced be-
ingness. Incorporating Zen principles from a feminist-centered perspective, as-
sertiveness techniques, and female-focused activities to assess each and every
woman's personal Hierarchy of Needs and establish a Power Grid for Loving
and Living, this workshop is being offered in conjunction with...

"Oestrogen poisoning," Grace muttered, and deleted the e-mail.

What had her sister been thinking, sending her this crap? Flora Trust
had lost her mind, no question about it. She'd gone off to live on a feminist
commune in Oregon. Grace suspected she had become a lesbian. Exposure
to too much tofu, too many cats, and too many women in Birkenstocks
would probably do it. Even a fucked-out, sperm-burping road whore
wouldn't be able to hang onto her heterosexuality in that environment.
Flora Trust had flirted with the idea of changing her name to something

53

more New Age: Crystalline, MariaDolphin, Starwomon. (To annoy her, Grace liked calling her Flora Trust Fund.) Their mother had extinguished that idea with one simple word: *inheritance*. Flora Trust kept her name true to her Deep South roots and kept herself mostly out of sight and out of mind, but – like a cold sore or a yeast infection – she still popped up now and then with irritating e-mails like these.

Grace generally had very little time for women who howl their radical feminist fuzziness at the moon. Maybe it had something to do with growing up in the rural South. Grace knew she waffled between wanting to be treated like the debutante she was, and wanting to claw her way to the front of the pack like any other affluent American exurbanite. She suspected these women's empowerment workshops attracted a bunch of braless frumps who were into crystal-worship, group crying sessions, and squatting naked over mirrors to look up inside their own parts.

"My vagina is beautiful!" Grace muttered again. "It's a rare and exotic orchid of love!"

When was the last time Rich had called it that? For that matter, when was the last time he had eaten her out? She couldn't remember. The only eating going on in this house lately had been Grace at the table, with food.

And the only eating out Rich was officially doing involved restaurants. Those long business lunches ("strategy sessions") with the partners. Rich ate out all the time lately. Trying to make partner meant he had to work around the clock. Of course, he had his women on the side and Grace knew perfectly well what went on between the sheets, but under this roof, things were different. At this rate she was going to dry up. She should have taken her mother's advice, found herself some illicit cock in Paris, and ridden it until she screamed. But men had the power to behave like that; women didn't, or at least not openly. Grace was trying to hold on to her husband and their home... the entire façade of their entire life together.

54

Gloria spoke up: *Power? When did you start thinking about the power, outside of your last visit to the fuse box? Honey, power is when the best-looking man in the room gets you your coat and holds the door for you when you have decided it's time to leave. Power is wrapping your husband around your finger and him begging you to tie the knot tighter. Power is understanding that men run the world, and behind the scenes, women run their men. We're in charge. You never understood that, and you of all people should have learned that lesson at an early age. But you let yourself go, and look where it's gotten you. Rich should have paid for that trip to Paris, reserved the bridal suite at the best hotel in town, and lavished you with money and attention. Instead, you chased after him like a pregnant hussy in a house coat and slippers…*

"Enough already," Grace said.

She'd been back from Paris a week. Rich got back two days ago. The most contact they'd had was the half-hour Grace spent watching him sleep this morning. She longed to touch him but was afraid to, not for fear of waking him up but of the look on his face when he recognized her. Whatever the name of the tramp he'd been waking up with in Paris, Grace had no doubt he smiled at her in the morning, no matter how messy her hair was, no matter how bad her breath smelled.

She stared out across their back yard. The gardener, Tony Lau, was working his way through Stanford at his father's lawn maintenance business. Tony would mow the grass, trim the hedges, weed and fertilize the flowers. Grace decided to have a second mimosa. She knew she shouldn't – alcohol is pure calories and sweetened fruit juice is almost as bad – but the morning was too warm for herbal tea, and she wanted to soften the start of her day with the emollient glow of peach schnapps. *Every sip's going straight to your hips,* Gloria cautioned. Grace watched Tony for a moment. Broad shoulders, narrow waist, solemnly handsome features. She wondered whether she could seduce him.

Grace did not want to be challenged. She wanted to stop the world and get off. She imagined a room in its own safely self-contained dimension, outside of time. When she felt sick or depressed – and this morning, she was definitely laboring in the fields of depression – she fantasized about retreating to this room. She knew the furniture by heart: a slightly shabby overstuffed blue sofa with her favorite pillow, a couple of extra cushions, and a warm wool throw to snuggle up under during the cooler months; a reclining armchair, similarly battered, with a spavined ottoman that didn't match; a mismatched pair of reading lamps; and a coffee table made from one of her grandfather's antique wooden sea chests. Grace's sanctuary also contained a large and lavishly appointed bathroom (soaking tub, shower stall, toilet, bidet, and more bath products than even Robert could dream of owning) and a bedroom empty except for a big four-poster bed, a night stand, and billowing white curtains at the windows. There was no kitchen because Grace's fantasy didn't require one: when she stretched out on her imaginary sofa or ate imaginary breakfasts in bed, food just appeared when she wanted to eat. And nothing was fattening.

She didn't want to fight for her marriage because she didn't feel she should have to. Rich ought to be fighting to keep her sane while she dealt with her weight. His job was important but he didn't wake up next to it. It didn't live and breathe and want to bear his children. She and Rich had gotten married, hadn't they? There had been something in the vows about *for better or for worse, in sickness and in health*, hadn't there? Even loosely interpreted, she felt a big ass ought to be covered by the bit about *'til death do us part*.

Flora Trust had once asked her: *What if you wake up one day and realize the kids are the only reason you and Rich still talk to each other?* Grace had not answered the question, but she had deflected it to Mary Rose. *What if you wake up one day and ask yourself, Is this all there is? Shouldn't*

56

there be more? Mary Rose didn't answer the question, either. She burst into another geyser of tears, and Grace dropped the subject. After a Valium, a vodka, and fifteen or twenty minutes, Mary Rose's wails and nose-blowing subsided.

Grace sometimes wondered what was left to salvage. Maybe the radioactive isotope of their relationship had its own half-life and nothing short of a spin through the particle accelerator on the other side of town would change that. When was the last time she and Rich had enjoyed a long conversation late into the night, with a bottle of wine and cheese and a box of their favorite onion crackers and meaningful looks into one another's eyes? Grace racked her brain to recollect the last time he had deigned to speak more than three sentences to her. All these philosophical questions were giving her a headache, and she didn't think it was just the alcohol from her second drink. What was she trying to preserve, if she was honest with herself?

An answer came: *everything.*

*

"Plan a big seduction scene for him," Robert said. "Put the whole day into it. Get yourself feeling sexy. Go to the spa and get every treatment they have. Spend a fortune at one of those upmarket grocery stores you like. Buy a new dress and a new bottle of perfume. Light a hundred candles and open a bottle of champagne. Get a massage and have the masseur stick his finger up your butt. I don't know. Maybe that's more my style than yours."

"The finger up the butt? Not big enough," Grace said. "I think an elbow or a leg would be more to your liking."

"Twat," Robert said.

"And don't you forget it. But let's make this about me, just for a little while? Not your voracious ass? What if Rich calls from work to say he's not going to be home until 11?" Grace asked. "Again?"

"Tell him if he ever wants to see your pussy again he'll get his ass home at a decent hour," Robert said. "If he gets there when you've already drunk the whole bottle of champagne, the candles have melted, and you're pissed off and crying, it won't do your relationship a goddamn bit of good."

Tears pricked at the corners of Grace's eyes. *My whole way of life, gone, just like that,* Grace thought. What she said, with effort, was, "But what if that's exactly what he wants? Not to see my..."

"Cunt," Robert helpfully offered.

"Again."

"Then you have to make sure you don't fuck this up," Robert said.

"How do I do that?"

"I know someone who can help. I've mentioned him before."

"Is he a liposuctionist with an industrial cellulite vacuum for my ass?"

"No, but he's the next best thing."

"Give me his number."

*

Grace didn't believe a word of it. Robert had always been a little gone around the bend over his friend James, she thought. Around the bend? No, it went farther than that. Over the river and through the woods. Somewhere out in orbit around Uranus. Somebody's anus.

Oh James, I want to lie next to you on a picnic blanket and stare into your eyes to see the fiery glow of the setting sun reflected in them. Oh James, I'd surrender my Y chromosomes if only I could, to give you beautiful squalling babies. Oh James, you break my heart every time you look at me and only see my flab instead of this tender and quivering soul that aches with love for you. Won't

58

you please fart in my presence, so I can take a deep whiff and tell you it smells like gardenias?

Grace loved Robert but at times he made her just the teeniest tiniest bit nauseated. James was not perfect or even necessarily Mister Right. No doubt he was very handsome and smart (in fact, just the sort of man Grace regretted not seducing in France, apart from the homosexuality, of course), and no doubt Robert had reason for being smitten, but after all this time, hadn't he gotten the hint? James didn't have romantic feelings for him. James didn't want to sleep with him. It was time to grow up and move on.

And now this. Stefan the supernatural Play Doh sculptor who could peel off the pounds by magically convincing the body it didn't need that extra hamburger, that quart of Ben & Jerry's, or that fifth glass of Beaujolais Nouveau. He sounded like the Santa Claus or Tinker Bell, a character only children believe in. Grace heard her mother's voice again: *Clap your thunder-thighs together if you believe! Do you believe, Gracie? Do you? Stefan the Magical Masseuse is depending on you, and if you don't clap those hocks of yours together, he just might disappear in a puff of pink smoke! Never to be seen again! Do you believe, Grace? Do you believe in life after flub?*

On the other hand, what if there was something to it? She indulged in a quick fantasy about being svelte without the miseries of exercise and dieting, then shoved those thoughts out of her head. It was too easy, too good to be true.

Grace wrote Stefan's phone number on the back of her phone bill, which was still in its envelope. Might as well pay bills this afternoon. She certainly wasn't going to call Mister Magic Fingers to schedule a weight-loss massage. She'd probably end up storming out of the session and getting dressed in his living room after he got a little fresh with her and grabbed a boob. (On the other hand, if Robert was seeing him, he was probably gay, and did she really want to undress in front of a man who not just didn't want her, but *didn't want her?*) But before she sat down to the onerous task of writing checks, she helped herself to another mimosa. And called her favorite travel agent to ask about medical-tourism vacation options in Latin America. Maybe she'd go to Costa Rica for a month: lipo and a tummy tuck, followed by a couple of weeks of therapeutic lounging on the beach. It would be just the thing – once the bandages came off, the drainage tubes came out, and she looked less like the survivor of a plane crash, she'd be a new woman. And Rich would never notice she was gone.

Gloria spoke up: *No, Grace, you are NOT running off to Panama to get your ass fat sucked out. You're going to stay right here and keep paying that detective to follow Rich around until you have so much evidence he won't be ABLE to leave. Whether you've turned into a butterball or not, he won't be able to leave you when you've got videotape of him eating a slice of some other woman's cherry pie, will he? Now get with the program!*

Grace drew a deep sigh. Some days, she wondered whether she should speak to someone about her mother's persistent psychic intrusions. This couldn't be healthy. It couldn't be a good sign. Grace wondered what these visitations were a symptom of, and whether there was a pill she could take to control them.

Tony Lau had finished with the yard and now he was crossing the lawn to knock on her door. He'd smile that charming smile of his and she'd feel all moist and squishy Down There just from the smell of him: sharp and male, but significantly less rank than Rich got after working up a sweat. With the scent of grass and earth hovering around him, he smelled a thousand times more enticing than the overpriced crap at Sephora. He'd smile when she tipped him ostentatiously, and his almond eyes would crinkle at the corners, the bare beginnings of laugh lines. How old was he, like 20? Max?

Maybe he's gay, Grace cautioned herself. *You are absolutely not to hit on him. Either he has a girlfriend already, or he likes guys. He's not available, not even for a recreational fuck. He's way too young. He's out of your league. Don't go there.*

"It looks beautiful, Tony," she told him. "Let me get my purse. There's Evian in the fridge, if you'd like a bottle. Help yourself, please. I'll be right back."

He kicked off his shoes before entering her house – a habit that charmed her silly – and she took her time trekking back to the bedroom to fetch him his money. She liked the thought of him in her living room. As much as Grace wanted her husband back, there was no denying the cuteness of Tony Lau. He'd have smooth balls like a ripe organic plum – purplish, lickable. Salty. Rich's were hairy. Lickable, too, but she kept having to pluck hairs off her tongue afterward. (How long ago had it been?) Rich could take forever to climax, but a college kid like Tony wouldn't last two minutes. Even less if she were to rim him.

Maybe he'd brush up against something and leave a smear of sweat behind. She'd rub her fingertips through the moisture and lick his salt off them.

That's the spirit, Gloria said.

Grace checked herself. Anything her mother rooted for was, at best, suspect.

I want Rich, Grace replied.

Have it your way then, babe.

*

There were two phone calls that morning: Mike and Flora Trust.

First, Mike:

"Hi, Grace. This is Mike. How are you doing?"

Well, my vagina is still quite moist from fantasizing about the gardener, which is nice but a little distracting. When I took a shower this morning I decided I couldn't stand the sight of my bathroom scale, so I hid it in the cabinet under the sink. My husband probably has VD from all the women he's fucking on the side. I want to die. Other than that, I'm great. You?

"Grace?" Mike asked.

"Sorry," Grace lied. "I was just swallowing the last of a glass of water. Excuse me. I'm great. How are you doing?"

"Just fine, just fine. It's a beautiful morning, I just had breakfast, and I thought I'd call and check in with you. How was Paris?"

"Very Gallic," Grace said.

"Never been there," Mike said. "Maybe one of these days I'll find myself a girlfriend. We'll have to go check it out. All that romance..."

Grace felt sure there must be a point to this. Any minute now, the point would appear. She thought it would be rude of her to suggest that he get to it, so she kept listening. He blathered on about the City of Dog Poo on the Sidewalks a bit longer and finally spat out what he had really called to say:

"Look, Grace, if there's some new angle you want to pursue, great. Financial transactions, maybe. Or I could try to find out if he's fathered any illegitimate children..."

"Oh my fucking God!" Grace slumped across the sofa. "Don't even suggest it!"

"Grace, a woman in your position has to look at every angle."

"Leave no stomach unturned," Grace said. She fanned herself with a copy of *Architectural Digest*, which Rich subscribed to but neither of them read. When was the last time she'd actually looked through an issue of *Conde Nast Traveler* or *Interview*? Any number of such upscale props adorned their home. Even now, when they barely saw each other, both purchased items that people like themselves ought to own.

"Right. Look under every rock, see if there's a big ugly centipede."

"Thank you for the pretty picture," Grace said. "What is it that you're trying to tell me?"

"I think we need to call it a day, Grace. I can keep tailing him for you. I can keep taking pictures and gathering evidence, but you've got more than enough. I don't have to tell you that California is a community-property state. He's worth a lot, and you'll get half."

"I'm worth more, and I don't want him to have it," Grace shocked herself by saying. "I just want him back."

"Then may I ask you to reconsider your approach? If you have to divorce him, after you've racked up so much evidence, you're going to weaken your own case. You'll have to conceal things, pretend you know about less than you really do. That could be tricky. Not to mention illegal. If it goes that far. Fuck it, look, what I'm trying to say is, I'm beginning to have some ethical struggles over this."

"You?" Grace asked. She stopped fanning herself. "What on earth is unethical about this, other than what Rich is doing?"

"If you were going to file for divorce, you would have done it by now. You're being wronged, but you're also being complicit in it. I can't help but feel I'm making things worse for you through my involvement. I'm sorry, but there it is. If you want to hire another detective, I can recommend several good ones, but I feel I've done as much for you as I can."

"I don't believe this," Grace said. The gyroscope of her mind wobbled; it threatened to stop spinning. She couldn't find words to describe the emotions roaring through her. She looked around the room, then looked out the window, then looked down at her lap. She needed to have the sapphire on her favorite ring reset. She needed a manicure. She needed to put gas in her car. And what the *fuck* was Mike talking about? "You're quitting. I thought you... I thought detectives were always... what do you want, more money?"

"It's not that," Mike said. "And I'm not hurting for work. I'm turning people away, to tell the truth. It's about ethics, and it's about knowing where to draw the line. You're a nice lady, Grace. You ought to give yourself a little more credit. You can do better than Rich."

"I don't think I can hear this right now," Grace said. "I don't think I can take it all in. I can't process it. I need some time. Let's talk later. Thank you."

She hung up on him.

Twenty minutes later, the phone rang again.

She almost didn't answer when she saw the Oregon area code on the Caller ID screen.

Flora Trust was probably calling to say she'd bought a new Saab. It was about time for one. She did that in odd-numbered years. For a muff-munching latter-day pagan, she was as reliable as clockwork in her way. Even before she replaced the license plates, she covered the ass end of each new car with bumper stickers, "for that lived-in look," as she put it. THE GODDESS IS ALIVE AND MAGICK IS AFOOT. VISUALIZE WORLD PEACE. VISUALIZE WHIRLED PEAS. And without fail, she slapped on the "random acts of senseless beauty" one that made Grace want a grenade launcher whenever she saw it on the back of somebody's SUV.

After their greetings, Flora Trust asked if Grace had read the e-mail about the power workshop.

"Honey, I know things with Rich haven't gotten any better."

"How would you know that?"

"I'm your sister. You have to ask?"

Grace hated when Flora Trust presumed to talk to her with the smugness of a much older and wiser sibling. She was older by five years, but not necessarily wiser. Grace struggled not to regress back to adolescence when

64

Flora Trust called and started pushing all the old buttons.

"Yes, you've known me since you were born, I know."

"How many mimosas have you had this morning?"

Shit, Flora Trust must have heard her pouring the orange juice.

"Nineteen. If I can still hear you after this one, I'm switching to heroin."

"I'm not going to do this dance with you, Grace."

"Flora Trust, I love you but if you called me up just to tell me how to act, I need to hang up the phone now. Okay? I'm a grown woman." Grace took a deep breath, then poured schnapps into her glass of OJ as quietly as possible. Did this make her an alcoholic? Or just unwilling to listen to more of her sister's bullshit? "I have things to do today. Hearing about how I drove my husband away because I didn't cut meat and alcohol out of my diet isn't one of them."

Grace didn't need to hear Flora Trust's shopworn litany of "big butt = personal failure" because she already believed it herself, even if she loudly proclaimed otherwise to anyone who would listen.

"I'm calling about the workshop." Flora Trust, unlike Mike half an hour before, got right to the point.

"Workshop?" Grace was used to the back-channel negotiations inherent to female communication and whenever her sister talked like a man, all bets were off.

"The one about reclaiming your life and your relationship?"

Oh, right. That. The Wiccans with mirrors. Group crying sessions. Herbal healing. Twat astrology. That.

"I don't think I…"

"Need to get a life?" Flora Trust's question slipped into Grace's mind like a lobotomist's swizzle stick.

"Why I…" Grace spluttered. No other words would come. She hung up on her sister, too.

65

CHAPTER SIX:

ROBERT

Subways. Collapsing parentheses. Sex in Saskatchewan.

Robert slid into the same trance the second time he visited Stefan. Was Stefan scooping handfuls of fat away from Robert's sides, or squeezing it out like pus from a monstrous zit? Adrift in the cerebral fog, Robert heard Stefan mutter under his breath. Like trying to follow dialogue on TV in the neighbor's apartment, Robert couldn't make out the words, just the tone. He was in his body and at the same time, he wasn't. He swam through the soup of a flashback: dissecting frogs in high school biology. The frog corpses, which the teacher ordered by the dozen (from a catalog Robert never, ever wanted to see), came with their internal organs injected with various dyes. When you cut their bellies open, you revealed an ugly formaldehyde rainbow: yellow liver, blue lungs, red heart, green intestines. What color were Robert's own organs? At one point Robert became convinced Stefan had found something ominous. Purple pancreas? Gold gall bladder? Fluorescent pink Islets of Langerhans?

Maybe he lost something in my guts last week. The image of a Timex ticking among the coils of his intestines was too disturbing to hold onto for long. He blacked out on the thought *It takes a licking and keeps on ticking, even when you drop it into a bath of stomach acid and e. coli.*

"There should be no more hair on your back and shoulders," Stefan said afterward.

"I could kiss your toes," Robert said.

"Help yourself," Stefan said. "I just had a pedicure."

Woozy, Robert sat up on the table. He thought it was a nice touch for Stefan to use cloth over his – what kind of table was it, exactly? A massage table? Operating table? Smorgasbord? In any case, Robert appreciated the silence of fabric instead of the humiliation of waxy paper crunkling under his butt during a visit to the doctor.

"Take your time," Stefan said. "Don't sit up too fast. I did a little more this time, and it'll take your body longer to adjust to the changes. You're not driving home today, are you? I will call you a cab."

Robert shook his head. "What do you think? I took the train this time." Rubbing his head as if a headache might be brewing, he said, more to himself than to Stefan, "In a normal city, there would be just one subway system and not two stacked on top of each other. People whose guts have been pulled out shouldn't be asked to switch train lines."

"In this country, a normal city would not have a subway, it would have a thousand miles of congested freeways. But you're feeling more alert. That's good. You'll come more fully awake in the next half-hour, and you'll be fine on the way home. I want you to go straight home and go to bed, though. You can eat a light meal if you're hungry, but don't overdo it."

"I thought you were giving me an appetite-ectomy."

Stefan handed Robert his underwear and T-shirt.

"I am, but let's call it a partial one. We're doing this in stages, remember. We want your body to adjust to the changes over time."

"So I won't want to eat the whole refrigerator when I get home?"

"No, just the front door and the hinges." Stefan smiled. "Can you get dressed?"

"I guess so. What else did you do?"

"If I told you everything, you wouldn't believe me. Plus, it would diminish the experience of discovering it for yourself. I took care of the back and shoulder hair. The back of your neck, too. It was unsightly. Now, no more waxing. I reconfigured a couple of your toenails to keep them from becoming ingrown. You smashed your pinky-toe when you were young, yes?"

Still naked, Robert nodded. One of his father's doomed attempts at bonding – a weekend sailing trip – had resulted in the broken toe. Robert, only 13 and already aware that he and his father would never be close, had tried to talk his way out of going, and the result was the closest to a temper tantrum he had ever seen his father throw. When one of his father's drunk sailing buddies dropped a heavy cooler full of Bud Lite on Robert's foot, the trip ended immediately. Despite the pain, Robert smiled with relief. His father didn't speak much while they waited in the emergency room. Their relationship never recovered. A year later, he was dead. Robert couldn't tell whether he missed the man or not, and his toe had never been quite the same, either.

This is my body. This is who I am. This hunk of moving, breathing meat is me. Robert sometimes had to remind himself he existed.

"It never grew back the right way. It was black in places, yes? And it was vulnerable to fungus. It needed to be fixed. When a fungus takes hold in the body, it can be difficult to eradicate."

"Even for you?"

"The body is stronger, but the fungus has to be convinced it would be happier elsewhere."

"Happier elsewhere? Where, like Puerto Vallarta?" Robert looked up at him. "You're joking, right?"

"I'm German. We don't have a sense of humor, remember?" Stefan smiled. "You also had a yeast overgrowth. Most Americans do, because

68

people in this country eat terrible food. Yeast is the hardest thing for me to eradicate from the system. Yeast colonies have a primitive intelligence. They can be quite argumentative. But you don't want to hear about my theories. In terms of difficulty to eradicate, yeast ranks alongside the virus and prion diseases, but I purged it from your system. It shouldn't come back. I cleaned up most of the leftover toxins, too. You'll feel much better in a couple of days' time."

Robert wouldn't know a prion if one came up to him on the street and said *hey baby*, but didn't think this needed pointing out.

Stefan asked, "Can you put on your clothes now or do you need me to dress you like a little boy?"

I might enjoy that too much.

"Then put on your underwear when you're ready. I'll get you a bottle of water. You'll need to pee in a couple more minutes, and when you get home, you'll need to go to the bathroom again. You may have a little diarrhea. Don't worry about it, it's just your body getting rid of those toxins and other things it doesn't need. But it won't happen until you're home. No bad surprises while you're on the train."

With effort, Robert stood up. "That's good to know."

"Are you almost ready?" Stefan asked. "You look like you're daydreaming. I hope they're nice daydreams. You're not about to fall asleep, are you?"

"No," Robert said. "I mean, yes I'm ready and no I'm not falling asleep. Just, you know, drifting, I guess."

Robert hurried back into his clothes.

Were his pants looser?

The question troubled him all the way home.

Seated, on the train, Robert couldn't very well shove his hand down his pants to measure his waistline or anything south of it. He needed to be standing for that. And he couldn't do it without attracting the wrong sort of attention. You couldn't walk a block down any Bay Area sidewalk without tripping over a drooling mental defective; nor could you ride a train without a Person With Mental Illness nearby muttering to him or herself, picking his or her nose, snoring in a stack of yesterday's newspapers, or playing a spirited game of pocket pool.

Robert inventoried bodily sensations as he did when he felt sick. Was his nose really getting stuffy or was it just the smog? And how about his throat? Had he been talking too much at work? Did it really hurt or was it more of a *discomfort*? Did he really have muscle aches, fatigue, and sore joints, or was he just sleep-deprived? Should he cut down on the red wine? Wasn't wine supposed to have beneficial properties? It must; the French would be a nation of immortals if it weren't for the buttery, cholesterol-laden shit they ate. Ergo, red wine must contain some preservative. Ergo, the red wine could stay. *Quod erat demonstrandum.* He probably wasn't sick. This is how his mental calculations usually went. And after the session with Stefan, Robert was doing the same thing:

I think I'm skinnier. I feel taut. I feel tingly. Sort of rosy. My belly doesn't feel as heavy. I don't feel as heavy. But it could be that I'm wearing new pants, and they're bigger in the waist. What would it be like to fit into a coach class seat on an airliner without feeling like I've been squashed in a trash compactor, at the end of the flight? Oh, wait, nobody above the age of twelve can ride in coach without feeling that way afterward. Fuck the airlines. I think I'm skinnier.

Robert feigned nonchalance and put off the naked self-inspection ritual as long as he could. He wanted to believe he possessed a measure of self-control. If he kept himself busy doing things – attacking the clutter on his desk and kitchen table, hand-washing the wine glasses he couldn't put in the dishwasher, scouring the sink, folding and putting away the basket of clean laundry he'd already resorted to picking socks and underwear out of, sorting bills into piles for Now and Next Paycheck – then he wouldn't have to confront how desperately he wanted to strip in front of the bathroom mirror. He could no more avoid it than a junkie could say no to a fix. He could only delay, and that was good enough for about an hour. He distracted himself by preparing a salad. Organic spinach, carrot slivers, celery, sunflower seeds, a dash of olive oil, a smaller dash of balsamic vinegar, ground pepper.

"Delicious, if you're a rabbit," Robert surveyed his work. His reward for eating it would be a glass or two of a cheerful Sonoma Merlot he'd discovered last week. "Why the hell not?" He sipped the wine, which had opened up beautifully, having been uncorked the night before. As soon as he'd drunk his inhibitions away, he'd shed his clothes too.

Robert sat at his table and stared into the salad as if he could read the vegetation like tea leaves. All that spinach suggested restraint, discipline, slenderness, iron. If he would just partake. And not order a pizza later.

"Oh, fuck it."

Robert left the plate on the table and dashed to the bathroom, unbuttoning his shirt along the way. He felt lighter, more nimble, as if his muscles had been tuned like guitar strings after a long interval of flatness. (*Fatness?*) He smiled. He'd heard people who join gyms experience a burst of energy after a good workout but two years ago when he'd signed up at 24 Hour Fitness, the only thing he'd taken away from his first and only three attempts at exercise was a grinding ache in his arms and legs that lasted about a week.

"What are your fitness goals?" the manager had asked, as they had filled out Robert's membership papers together.

The manager was a bald, black, and muscular version of Mr. Clean, down to the big gold hoop earring in his right ear. Nerdy black-framed glasses over an impishly handsome face. Biceps like boulders. Robert remembered wanting to see him naked. Maybe there would be fringe benefits to this exercise thing after all.

"Did you notice my stomach when I walked in? That's my fitness goal."

Now, Robert tossed the shirt across his bathroom counter and pulled off his T-shirt next. Something crashed to the floor – his deodorant – not broken – fuck it. Robert had a long habit of avoiding his reflection in the mirror. Above the neck, he didn't mind so much. Although his body tended toward the proportions of a woman in her eighth month of pregnancy, he didn't have a bad face, and men's faces do require shaving. The prospect of undressing, though, lined his belly with dread.

Robert's gut was still present and accounted for. But there didn't seem to be as much of it. His eyes didn't trace the same arc along his waist.

He stepped out of his trousers. They slid to the floor with a whisper that became a thump when his belt landed in the heap of cloth. His heart raced and his bowels felt full. Right, Stefan told him to expect that. Next step, the underwear. Another agonizing daily ritual, the terrible moment of naked truth.

He wanted to call James. James hadn't been making this shit up. Robert wanted to scream "You were right" and "Look at this!" and "See how much better I look already!"

The underlying question was, "Do you like me yet?"

He turned to view himself from every angle. He still had a gut but it didn't jut out as far. His buttocks looked less like a large set of collapsing parentheses and more like... well, buttocks. His back, not hairy now, shocked him. In addition to removing the tufts of hair, Stefan had thinned out the galaxy of moles by at least an Orion and a Big Dipper.

"One day," Robert said out loud, "I'm going to have... *obliques!*"

He spun around like a runway model, lost his balance, and tumbled against the wall. Then had a good laugh at his own giddy stupidity. His next thought was, *I have got to start getting laid. Without paying for it.*

*

When Grace showed up at Dufferin & Smuck the next day with a duffel bag of clean shirts and underwear for Rich, he barely spoke to her. Robert met her at reception and escorted her in because the prick wouldn't answer his personal phone line. In Rich's office, Robert kept his face a careful blank and saw his sister doing the same thing. *Hmm, we must be related or something.* She barely spoke to her husband, in return – although Robert could tell she wanted to scream.

Rich put in obscene hours at the office, to Grace's keen dissatisfaction. Rich and a couple of other lawyers would sometimes stay in hotel rooms for days on end. Robert knew what else they got up to because they made no real effort to hide it – Rich's disregard and near-contempt for Grace were not exactly secrets at the office. Rich would take off an hour a day, usually late in the afternoon, for a trip to the gym and a hasty meal. Sometimes longer, if he'd made plans with one of his women. Either way, he'd return glowing and pumped. He'd work like a machine until well into the night, cab over to his hotel, and sleep in his clothes.

They stopped by Robert's office afterward.

"This isn't a marriage," she said.

"Doesn't look like one," Robert said.

"You should get back to work."

"They stay at a cheap place on Nob Hill," Robert said. "It has an Indian name. I can't remember it."

Grace nodded. "I know which hotel it is."

"You still want him back."

She sighed. A very young paralegal in an oversized shirt and trousers and a badly knotted blue necktie scooted past the doorway, carrying a foot-thick stack of manila folders.

"That kid didn't give me a second look," Grace said. "Ten years ago, he would have. Yes, I want him back."

"Ten years ago, I'd have gotten the second look, not you," Robert said. He looked after the kid. The cuffs of his trousers dragged the floor. He absently hiked them up after stepping on the fabric with the heel of one of his Doc Martens. A braided belt about eight inches too long cinched the pants around a very skinny waist, but Robert caught a glimpse of broad shoulders. Without that detail he'd look skeletal; you couldn't pick a lock with him but you could almost put both hands around his waist.

But I make six figures. I bet he can barely make rent, if he lives in the city. Who's better off?

"I think he bats for my team and not yours. Although ten years ago he was still sperm in his daddy's sac."

"I have to go," Grace said. "Nothing personal. Let's talk later, okay?"

After Grace left, Robert returned to his office with a leaden sense of resignation. What would it be like to drop everything and run, billable hours be damned? All he had to look forward to was a long afternoon plowing through three-inch-deep document after four-inch-deep document after five-inch-deep document. His eyes ached in anticipation. A headache thrummed like concert speakers during a sound check. Robert sat down, took off his reading glasses, shoved the stacks of documents aside, called James, and said "Meet me at the Metro at 7.00 sharp. Not negotiable. If you have plans, cancel them. We're going flesh-hunting."

"You actually want to go to the Castro?"

"Lots of impossible things are happening lately. Why not add another to the list?"

"How many times have you seen Stefan?" James asked.

Robert wondered if James was still seeing the doctor with the Audi and the incandescent grin. Whether the doctor had noticed the change below James's waist. What do you do in a situation like that? When your partner brushes your question aside with a smile and an innocuous remark like *I've been taking my vitamins*, which was the kind of thing James would say? Do you tell yourself you must have been wrong the first time around? Do you put up with the cognitive dissonance? Or accept the new and improved appendage as is, go down on it with a happy slurp, and rejoice in your sore throat the next morning? Some questions will never be tackled by the philosophers, but should be.

"Twice."

"And?" James sounded weary but not skeptical.

"And. I'm a piece of shit. You were right all along. You were always right. You're bigger where you wanted to be. I'm smaller where I wanted to be. The change isn't huge but I can tell. Today when I took a break for lunch, I went to Macy's and bought clothes."

"Smaller ones?"

"Well, I didn't have to shop in the children's section..."

"But you're happy with the results."

"Very."

"Have people at work noticed?"

"One of the secretaries asked if I was working too many hours," Robert said. "I told her I've been watching what I eat, and she said *Don't tell anyone, but Jenny Craig and I are having a lesbian affair!* She made a V with two fingers and stuck her tongue through the vertex. Doesn't it just break your heart?"

"I'm crying," James said. Was he busy or was he being cold? "I can meet you tonight but I can't stay long. I'm meeting the doctor for a late dinner, and sleeping over."

"Still seeing him, then?" Robert analyzed his feelings. He took the usual, predictable blowtorch flame of jealousy for granted. He expected it, like death and taxes. But he felt *lighter*, and that mitigated his jealousy somewhat. How much did toxins weigh, anyway? Did toxic fat weight more than the regular kind? Were toxins like little sacks of fertilizer secreted in cellular rental trucks, waiting to blow something important to bits?

"Yes, which you'd know if you'd been talking to me." Robert winced to hear James sound so bitter, and pushed the thought *I'm the cause of that* out of his head as soon as it formed there. As a lawyer, Robert reminded himself not to make assumptions about cause and effect.

"I've been a shit, James. I'm not going to pretend otherwise." Robert took a deep breath. "I've been unhappy with myself and you've caught the brunt of it. It's easier to see now that…"

"It's all right," James said. "I understand. I referred you to Stefan, after all. Remember?"

"How could I forget?"

"And I'm not even mad at you for… you know."

"I deserve it," Robert said.

"Well, I kind of opened the door."

"The zipper, more like."

"Christ, now I need a drink."

"Hey, it wasn't *that* bad," Robert said. He prayed James wouldn't say *Yes it was, actually.* "But we don't need to go there again. Let's have a drink or three. You go play doctor afterward, and I… I'm feeling confident. I may even get laid."

"Without paying anybody," James said. "If I didn't think Stefan could work miracles before, I do now."

"Oh, fuck you."

"Oh, I'll be getting fucked tonight, but not by you. See you at seven?"

Without waiting for an answer, James hung up on him.

76

*

I'm going to get myself fired, Robert thought.

He looked at the stack of paper on his desk and wondered how important the contracts could possibly be. Important enough to be worth several hundred million dollars, yes, but he couldn't read another page of fine print without his eyeballs falling out and dangling from their stalks like wet yo-yos.

He buzzed Jennifer, his secretary. In his best authoritative voice, he said, "I'm taking off the rest of the afternoon. Got a couple of things to do. If anybody calls, tell them I'm in a meeting. I'm turning off my cell."

On the way out, she looked as if he'd announced plans to move to Rwanda.

He quelled an urge to explain himself: *Yes, I want to make partner, preferably before Rich does. But we all want things we can't have, and the mind and body can only abide tedium for so long. Law school builds stamina but hating the way you look wears it down again. And I'm fried. I know you've noticed how much better I look. I've caught you checking me out. Don't lie, Jennifer. It's not a sexual thing but you know I've lost weight and you want to know how. Right now the most important thing on earth is to get the fuck out of this office and try out my new and improved bod in the same bars I've spent most of my years in the Bay Area avoiding. When the pounds change, so do the priorities. The only briefs I want to see today are the ones under some guy's pants.* He wanted to say those things but kept his mouth shut. He stared back at her long enough that she probably figured some of them out for herself.

She's my secretary, not my mother, Robert reminded himself. The idea of having Gloria for a secretary filled him with horror. Her enmeshment issues would reach legendary new levels. He walked out of the office at a brisk pace, not running but doing his damnedest to evince purpose and

77

direction, while also avoiding eye contact. When the building's heavy glass front doors whooshed shut behind him, he deflated in relief. A waiting taxi would cap the moment off perfectly but the subway would be faster.

Robert shivered in the cold midsummer wind.

Only in San Francisco, he thought.

How much did Jennifer know about him, anyway? How long could you work in the same office with someone without gleaning even the most basic facts? Sure, she knew he was gay; everyone did. She probably knew he was single. Until recently he had been putting in killer hours, minus the performance art other attorneys made of cuckolding their significant others, Rich being the prime example. The only partner on Robert's mind had been the kind that meant he'd gotten a promotion. More money, less work, and a better office. Jennifer didn't know he liked subways, for example, nor that he spoke fluent German and passable French. She didn't know he ate frozen pizzas three nights a week because cooking for one was too goddamn depressing, and leftovers always molded in his refrigerator.

How much did Stefan know about him now?

Robert shivered again. He looked up and down Market Street and felt trapped in the moment. A crumpled newspaper page rolled down the sidewalk toward him like a tumbleweed, caught on his trouser leg, then blew away in another gust of wind. Near the entrance to the Montgomery BART and Muni station several yards away, two homeless people of indeterminate sex huddled under drab bluish-grey blankets. All Robert could see of them were two human-sized lumps, some hair, and a single hand stretched out from under the fabric, jingling a Styrofoam cup of loose change.

This city.

How much did Stefan know? Robert walked absently toward the stairs at the entrance to the subway station. Stefan knew what Robert looked like naked but so what, so did anyone who'd seen him change clothes at the gym. Stefan knew intimate things about Robert's body even his doctor couldn't know – the toenail fungus, the yeast overgrowth, the moles and the hair on his back, the color of his guts.

How much damage could a body sustain and continue to function? Robert looked down at the hairy forearm jingling the cup of change. He thought of men and women blown apart in war. He thought of his own body: all that added weight – and he wasn't nearly as fat as some poor bastards he saw waddling down the street, every step a struggle against gravity. Maybe he had diseases and syndromes he didn't even know about – diabetes, hypoglycemia, incipient tumors, rare cancers, multiple sclerosis and psoriasis and Alzheimer's all waiting to bubble to the surface and reduce him to a pile of inert meat. But how much could he withstand without dropping?

"Christ, I need a drink," he said out loud.

"Don't we all?" said the bag lady standing next to him.

She held out her hand.

Horrified, Robert hurried downstairs into the Muni section of the underground station to catch a train, or fling himself in front of one, whichever seemed like a better idea at the time.

*

And so it came to pass that Robert got laid.

A boy – he was 25 but anyone that fresh-faced and innocent-looking still deserved to be called a boy – named Don overheard Robert telling James, "I want to piss on my boss's feet in the restroom."

"Don't we all?" Don said. He introduced himself and offered to shake hands with them both.

79

Robert looked at him and felt his face go tense, as if he were waiting for Don to say something dismissive before turning his attention to James. His type always did. The moment passed. Robert wondered why James hadn't pointed him out, and why Don had glommed onto them of all people.

He must want James, Robert thought. *He's the cute one.*

"Do we?" James asked.

Don seemed to be ignoring him. He asked Robert "Why do you want to pee on your boss's foot?"

"Well, I'd also be okay with pissing on his calves and knees. You know how it arcs. I wouldn't want to be so close to him that I'd be pissing on his thighs. That would be too weird. Below the knees is good enough..."

James interrupted: "Robert, he asked *why*, not *where*."

"Because I've been feeling good about myself lately?" Robert tried it out, to see how it would sound.

"Self-esteem is important," James said.

"You don't like your boss?" Don asked. "Or you don't like your job?"

A roar drowned out their conversation for a minute: the F-Market streetcar rumbled by. Robert knew from the racket it was one of the antique orange trams the Municipal Railway had obtained from Milan. They made twice as much noise as the other trolleys used on that line.

"I'm getting burned out," Robert said. "I didn't realize it until recently. I work at a law firm..."

"Say no more," Don said. "Let me guess. You've been working 80 hours a week for the last three or four years, and one day you looked up and asked *What happened to my life? Why did I put myself in debt to live like this? How did I delude myself into believing it would be worth it in the end? Am I close?*"

"Well, yeah, basically." Robert didn't need to add *And my magic massage therapist has been scooping the pounds off my flabby ass like rice from the*

80

bulk bins at the grocery store. Some truths are better not revealed until more drinks have been had.

Don stood about 5 foot 9, had sandy brown hair, slightly tousled, and was thin. Blue or grey eyes – Robert couldn't tell. It was too dark in the bar for details like that to be evident. Don's cheekbones soared like the vault of St Paul's Cathedral in London. Robert wanted to kneel and worship. He began to wonder if he wasn't going to get his chance. He was the object of Don's attention, not James.

That's a first.

Don, a tourist from Saskatchewan, was driving to Los Angeles to meet his brother's new fiancée. "I've never driven down the coast, you know? So I drove to Vancouver and turned south."

James asked, "Were you sleepless in Seattle?"

"No, I was more clueless and hopeless. Ever tried to drive in downtown Seattle? It's all, you know, vertical hills and one-way streets. Then there's the water, right there next to the city core, and the mountains beyond it – I can't tell you how many times I almost rear-ended the car in front of me."

Don ended his sentences with a charming upward lilt. He sounded vaguely Scottish. Robert imagined parents from Aberdeen or Inverness.

"Then I went to Portland. I liked it more than I expected to. I was expecting nothing but rain and lumber mills, but it's big! But I didn't stay long, though, because I wanted to see San Fran," Don said. "You know, Mecca?"

"And you've just rolled into town today, and don't even have a place to stay yet, right?" James asked, with more sarcasm than Robert thought necessary.

Don blushed and swirled the ice in his gin and tonic. It glowed sky blue under an ultraviolet light.

"Ever wonder why you don't pee fluorescent blue after drinking gin and tonic?"

"I don't usually take pisses under fluorescent lights," James said.

"We could take 'em out right here and pee," Robert offered. "Then we'd find out."

"It's almost time for me to meet..."

"The doctor?" Robert finished for him.

James excused himself and left in a hurry.

He's jealous, Robert realized. *Because for the first time in our acquaintance, I'm the one getting the attention. He can't handle it.* A minute later, another thought followed: *I could get used to this.*

When Don said, "I like men with some meat on their bones, you know? Skinny muscle boys don't do it for me at all," Robert thought someone had slipped one or both of them some kind of drug.

He wanted to ask Don, *What are you saying? You can't mean you didn't want to go get naked with James. Didn't you get a good look at him? That grin? I look like something you'd find under a rock in the woods. The only difference is I'm not chitinous and I have fewer legs.*

Then he shifted on his stool. The rustle of unfamiliar fabric reminded him of the new trousers he'd bought. The smaller waistline. The additional room in his shirts, and the way he'd needed three tries to knot his necktie at a length consistent with the new topography of his stomach.

I don't look too bad, really, he thought.

He had to keep reminding himself of that as Don drove them out of the Castro and across the slow-moving Bay Bridge toward Oakland.

"Can you believe these houses? All up next to each other like that? And the street people panhandling on every corner. Is it like that everywhere here? Don't you become numb to it after a while?"

"That's the thing about the Bay Area. It's beautiful here, but there's also a dense concentration of human misery. It's a paradox. Take that exit."

In the apartment:

"I like your place. Is it expensive to live here?"

"Outrageous," Robert said. "I don't know why I stay. Except for the fact that I live here, and I don't know where else to go."

"You're going to let me stay the night, right?" Don asked, changing the subject so fast Robert's head spun.

"Good way to save money on hotels," Robert commented.

Don nodded. His eyes twinkled. "I'm just a nice prairie boy from Canada," he said. "I don't know what you're talking about."

"Then let's see those great Canadian plains of yours on my bed, all right?"

CHAPTER SEVEN:
GRACE

The disease of the week. The zocalo. Your friendly neighborhood gym.

Things Grace tried, to lose the weight and keep it off:

Atkins. How could anyone be expected to survive without alcohol, desserts, and baked goods for more than two weeks without going insane? These diets spread like new strains of the flu. Just when you thought you'd been immunized, a new one would come along and everyone in town would succumb. She resigned herself to the knowledge that she'd try the next craze, too. And the one after that. And the one after *that*. She'd lose five pounds and gain back seven. And so it went: forward, backward, backward, forward…

Vacations in Mexico. Walking around all those historic plazas and exotic ruins, not to mention drinking all that untreated water, ought to have melted the pounds away, but didn't. No matter how charming the local *zocalo* was, no matter how far off the tourist trail they strayed, Grace wanted to come home with her fashionably gaunt figure the focus of everyone's attention, not the fact that yet again, she'd gone on a trip and not bothered to send postcards. It would have been more practical to break into a biology lab at Stanford and slurp the diseased agar agar out of a few Petri dishes, but where's the fun in that? Might as well lick the floor of a public restroom or suck the dried goo off the side of a Dumpster. In Mexico, she ate whatever she felt like eating: pastries from street vendors, salads in cheap restaurants, buffet food that had been ossifying under heat lamps for unimaginable stretches of time. She drank tap water by the gallon and would have given herself an enema with it but for the bother and mess. Dysentery eluded her and flattened Rich. *What I wouldn't give to have your iron stomach,* he told her once, sweaty and green in Manzanillo. *And what I wouldn't give to have yours,* she replied. He glared at her. She told herself it was just his fever talking when he said *The worst thing is, I believe you.*

Domestic disease options. Several years ago, a friend in Seattle had caught salmonella after eating at a cheap take-out teriyaki place, and had lost five pounds in two days. Grace thought a few hours on the commode and some chills might be worth the benefits to her figure and coaxed the name and address of the restaurant out of her still-groaning friend. She flew up to Seattle first class, checked into a hotel, forced down four execrable meals at the specified location, and had nothing to show for her efforts except for a stomachache and some gas. Seattle itself, she liked well enough: the snow-capped mountains and various bodies of water surrounding the city afforded stunning vistas wherever she looked. But the Third World offered her better chances of contracting an effective disease. No matter where she went, microbial exotica evaded her... and knocked Rich on his ass, all three subsequent times he accompanied her to Latin America, before he gave up on leisure travel (and their marriage) altogether. Grace wondered if she should try a different country: Nepal, India, Nigeria, Chad. Maybe Morocco, there to re-enact *The Sheltering Sky* by going slightly nuts in the Sahara as obscure (but slimming) fevers set in. But she never got around to it.

Lipo. She selected a doctor, underwent the obligatory consultation, made the appointment... and canceled at the last minute, forfeiting a deposit large enough to buy jewelry but quaking with relief. Surgery terrified Grace. Just imagining someone cutting her skin, inserting a cannula, and vacuuming out her fat deposits was enough to turn her legs to rubber. She'd ruled out stomach-stapling for the same reason. She needed to lose a pound or two (or sixty) but not if it involved being cut open. Now and then she fantasized about slashing her belly with a meat cleaver and shoving her Dustbuster into the wound, but Gloria always intervened whenever Grace eyed the knives for that extra fraction of a second.

Xenadrine, Hydroxycut, and other supplements. These left her jittery and irritable, borderline psychotic at times. (Not that she'd say no to trying a new one.) Her blood sugar veered and surged like a drunk driving home from happy hour. After a month on the pills that promised everything but offered little beyond a lethal mix of caffeine and ephedra, she fell apart. She'd lost ten pounds but couldn't shake the jitters and the tension headaches. She ground her teeth and clenched her jaw. Thoughts pingponged around inside her cranium, never still, and she understood why crazy people bashed their heads against the wall. *Keep this up,* her doctor intoned, *and you're going to develop TMJ. Assuming you don't have a stroke first.* Her period started late, and the cramps almost killed her. The diarrhea she couldn't seem to catch in Mexico bugged her almost daily. Her guts hurt. She couldn't trust her body. The day she blacked out in the Whole Foods parking lot, she decided enough was enough. She dumped the pills in the trash, their plastic bottle in the recycling bin next to it, then marched into the store and bought a chocolate cake, a dozen peaches, miscellaneous pears, a quart of the tequila-lime sorbet she loved, an entire roasted chicken, a bottle of cranberry-cherry juice, a baguette, a tub of French butter, some Brie, a white Bordeaux, a white Rioja, and six bottles of red. She ate half the baguette in the car on the way home and washed it down with organic chinotto. Too decadent. Back home, she finished the baguette in the driver's seat of her car, crumpled up the wrapper, and tossed it into one of the grocery bags. So much for Xenadrine. Bring on the Valium, baby, and let's wash it down with Merlot.

Diuretics. There's a limit to how many times a day it's okay to pee. Period.

Overeaters Anonymous. Fine, if you don't mind a diet of cognitive dissonance and fundamentalism in drag. The meetings were uncomfortably redolent of down-home, big-haired Southern religion. With a tent, some hymnals, a little heat prostration, and a box of rattlesnakes, the difference would be impossible to detect. Grace went to a meeting and left thinking *Their logic is even more circular than I am on my Fat Days*. Come to meetings so you won't eat. If you eat, you should come to more meetings. And by the way, you're probably also an alcoholic, an impulsive spender, a coke fiend, a pothead, and a slut. Addiction is insidious, and once it gets ahold of you, you're fucked.

*

The gym hadn't worked out, either. Not the last time, nor the time before that, nor the time before *that*. *This time, everything will be different*, Grace promised herself. Famous last words. *With the next man, everything will be different. With the next diet, everything will be different.* If you had any doubts, just pick up a women's magazine.

No, this time, it wasn't just about losing those extra pounds because that's what you were supposed to do these days. Every other Hollywood celebrity whose star had gone supernova a decade ago could now be found on daytime TV hawking exercise gear in fuzzy-lensed infomercials. The diet section at Long's Drugs occupied as much space as the pain relievers and cold remedies put together, and you couldn't walk down the center aisle without knocking over a Pilates mat and exercise ball combo in a box, yours for just $29.95. This time, Rich was probably leaving, and there was nothing she could do about it except to *lose weight.*

Excuse me, Grace, honey, but what's this "probably" horse shit? What's this "nothing you can do about it" load of bull? He's already gone. Which part of that doesn't make sense to you? Your husband is gone. He's out fucking every piece of tail he can stick his dick into, and you're still telling yourself you might have a little problem-y-poo? Either you whip your ass into shape and bring your marriage back from the dead, or you should be a good sport and pay for the divorce proceedings out of your own pocket. If you really want to be a grown woman about it, buy his next bimbette the engagement ring.

"I need to make a plan."

Having spoken the words aloud, Grace felt better, as if her sinuses had cleared after a lingering cold.

Nothing she could do about it? *Bullshit.*

"I am powerful. I can do this. It's not like I have a job to show up for." She looked around her immaculate living room and thought, *I need a drink.*

She could hire a trainer at the gym, and her doctor could recommend a nutritionist. She'd spend a fortune on cute workout gear, toss out everything of suspect caloric benefit in the fridge and the pantry, and fill the house with raw veggies and low-carb nutrition bars. She'd take walks. Living in Palo Alto, how could anyone justify not taking walks? Now she'd have an excuse to zip down to the Stanford Shopping Center for new walking shoes. One or two pairs, to be on the safe side. She'd get her hair restyled, spend a day at the spa, make a point of looking hot. Within a couple of weeks, Rich would notice the results. He'd want her again.

It would work.

It couldn't not work.

Don't be too sure, Gloria warned. *You've got to hold onto your power and your dignity. Any woman who forgets that is asking for trouble.*

"For fuck's sake, will you get out of my goddamn *head?*" Grace stared out the window. The yard looked resplendent, worthy of vacationing nobility. She wanted to take off her clothes and roll around in the new-mown grass. Perhaps with Tony Lau. Not that she'd do it – she didn't want bugs and grass clippings in her coochie – but the thought held a lurid appeal. "Damn, I'd almost think you want me to fail before I even get started!"

Gloria had nothing to say, but Grace could feel her hovering somewhere just over the psychic horizon, like a storm front or impending bad news.

She called Robert immediately, got his voice mail, left a message: "All right, you win. The seduction is on. Just don't expect me to go see your *X-Files* liposuctionist, okay?"

*

Entering the gym, Grace felt a quiver in her bowels. Behind the front counter, two waif-like girls in matching purple logo shirts stared at her as she walked in. The look on their faces suggested she had an extra set of breasts or a second head.

They're just looking, Grace reminded herself. *Women check each other out. It's a fact of life.* And it was. When you're 22 and have a darling figure, of course you're going to look at a chubby thirtysomething with a mixture of pity and smug contempt on your face. At least for a nanosecond, until the big warm orthodontically pristine smile your corporate-overlord training video tells you to zap customers with takes over.

Grace wondered what their names were. They weren't wearing name tags. *Bimba,* she thought. *The blonde one's name is Bimba and the black girl's name is Delicia.* They both looked so pert and fit and wholesome, Grace wanted to set their hair on fire.

"Hi!" Delicia smiled as if she meant it. "Are you new to the club?"

Grace nodded. She closed the distance to the counter, acutely aware of the whisking sound of her thighs brushing together.

Zzzz! Zzzz! Zzzz! Went the nylon.

Shit! Shit! Shit! Went Grace's inner voice.

Dance music pounded from hidden speakers, and weights clanked together. She heard grunts and gasps. Panting. With different lighting and worse music, this could be a porno movie set.

The pounding of feet on treadmills, mutters and exhalations from people straining under weights, lockers slamming shut, cardio machines beeping and whirring, overly shrill cries of encouragement from an aerobics instructor – these all added up to cacophony. If gyms were intended to counteract stress, why did they all have to be so goddamn loud?

"I need to sign up," she said. She shifted her gym bag from her left shoulder to her right and absently wiped her damp palms against her hips to dry them. The fabric of her track suit didn't absorb the moisture, though; it only redistributed it, with that same *zwish-zwish* sound her thighs made when she walked.

Two absurdly muscular men brushed past Grace on their way out. One had a goatee and one didn't; otherwise they were indistinguishable. The sweet rank sting of male sweat wafting in their wake pierced her through – when was the last time she had been close enough to Rich to catch that scent pouring off his body?

"Have you been a member of a gym before?" Delicia asked.

Grace nodded.

Overwhelmed, she'd have also nodded if Delicia had asked her whether she ate small children on a regular basis.

"Here, I've got a registration form for you," Bimba said. She handed Grace a clipboard. "Just sit down and fill that out."

"What about the hard sell?" Grace asked. "Last time I joined a gym, there were all these fees up front, and then this guy sat down and tried to sell me a package deal with supplements and like, a dozen sessions with a personal trainer..."

Bimba and Delicia exchanged a look. Grace couldn't read it: amusement? Puzzlement? Contempt?

"We're your friendly neighborhood gym, not the evil corporate one that just wants your money," Bimba said.

A quasar of hope ignited within Grace's breast. She'd expected suave fitness alligators in identical polo shirts. She'd expected to be openly snubbed before the door had swung shut behind her. These girls were being nice. Before Gloria could intervene and shut her up, Grace asked, "Why the warm reception? I honestly wasn't expecting it."

"If we were mean to everybody that didn't look like an Olympic athlete, nobody would come back, would they?" Delicia smiled again. "You're supposed to enjoy your workouts. They're supposed to make you feel good. Why screw it up for people? We're just glad you're here."

Grace wanted to cry.

The planets were finally lining up in her favor.

She was going to get Rich back.

"You've made my day," she said, trying not to let them see her well up, which she was doing entirely too often these days. (Thank God she wasn't wearing make-up. The embarrassment from black streaks of eyeliner leaking down her cheeks would kill her. But then, she'd never understood women who wear make-up to the gym.) "Where do I sign?"

*

Grace knew how to use fitness equipment because of her previous failures to establish an exercise routine. She liked the recumbent bike. You sat in it. How hard was that? She could do the bike for ten minutes and walk on the treadmill for fifteen. She could do a couple of sets of curls with dainty five-pound weights, and use a few of the less complicated machines without assistance. She also knew that for the next three days, she'd ache in places that weren't appropriate to mention in polite company.

She tried to think positive thoughts: *I shouldn't beat myself up for looking this way. I shouldn't hate that skinny girl two treadmills down, even though she looks like a skeleton in Spandex and she's running at full speed and I can smell her from here. We're all on different paths. We all got dealt different cards.*

For a few minutes, she actually believed herself.

Showering at the end of the workout was Not An Option. Grace gathered up her things and drove home, contemplating how Flora Trust would have walked brazenly around the locker room in the nude, chatting with complete strangers and even commenting on their bodies. *You've just got the most adorable figure!* Or, *Honey, I know that tattoo had to hurt going on. Booby-flesh is just so sensitive that close to the nipples! I just couldn't do it, and besides, these things are halfway down to my knees already, so why bother!* She took after their mother that way. Neither one of them would know a boundary if you garroted them with it.

Grace had a few hours left until sunset. She felt good about herself, optimistic, pleasantly flushed. Once home, she took a shower and changed into fresh clothes right away. Rich tended to wander around the house stinking after his trips to the gym, which Grace didn't actually mind. (It was kind of hot.) She needed to be clean and had shower gel in four or five scents to go with different moods. (Today was vanilla.) She poured herself a glass of iced rooibos tea and twisted a lemon wedge over it, then stepped outside to sit on the terrace and watch the color of the sky deepen.

The best antidote to depression is activity. Whenever she thought too much about losing Rich and the upheaval that would bring to her life, her blood turned into fine grey ash in her veins. Every muscle went flaccid. Her chest tightened; she struggled to breathe. By making a plan of attack, she allowed a small ray of hope into the gloom. She could do this. She could get through this. She could forget she'd ever seen those photos of Rich in bed with other women, and they could rebuild a life together. The Clintons had done it, hadn't they? Publicly? She and Rich could too. This pervasive emotional pall would recede into distant memory. She'd have reasons to get out of bed in the morning. She'd reflect on those long-ago moments when she couldn't seem to draw enough oxygen into her lungs, take Rich's hand, and offer up a tiny prayer of thanksgiving.

Two more weeks, and I'm winning him back, she promised herself. *Just two more weeks. I can do this.*

She got up to check the refrigerator for celery. Finding none, she decided to sack the nearest grocery store.

A shopping run to Palo Alto always brought Grace into contact with middle-aged women in track suits, glowing from a game of tennis or a nice 10-mile run. This time, the entire Stanford swim team, or their clones, appeared to be purchasing everything that wasn't nailed down: enough beer and food for a marauding army of Vikings, plus two carts full of toilet paper for purposes she didn't even want to guess at. Grace flash-fried her brain with a quick fantasy about doing every single one of the swimmers. After practice one day, she'd walk naked, slender, and goddess-like into the locker room and say *Make me your bitch.* Most of them were probably straight. The sight of all those horny boys fucking would get the gay ones worked up; it would be kind of hot to watch them doing each other while their teammates worked her over and peed on her breasts afterward.

Attagirl, Gloria said. *Remind me to tell you about my last trip to Cuba.*

Maybe some other time, Grace thought back at her. She looked at the swimmers again. *No, really, I just want Rich back.*

She grabbed half a dozen blood oranges, a bunch of celery, and a couple of cans of Wolfgang Puck's organic chicken soup for dinner. Rich wouldn't be home and (for now) could go fuck himself. Let him order take-out.

That's the spirit!

Grace wished her mother would shut up.

Standing in line at the check-out counter behind Grace were two men, both also strong contenders for pornographic fantasy: one sort of Latin, the other Japanese if her Bay Area Asian radar was working today. When she looked down at a magazine on the lowest rack, she saw the Latino had his arm around the Asian's waist. So much for her lurid fantasies.

"Taro, we forgot shiitake mushrooms." Nice voice this guy had, sort of Southern, which she noticed right away, and when Grace looked up, he had the oddest golden eyes.

"*You* forgot the shiitake mushrooms," Taro said.

He rolled his eyes at Grace when his boyfriend hurried toward the produce section, which looked as denuded as if a plague of locusts had been at it. Those swimmers and their appetites. She couldn't imagine how much their bill came to, and who was paying for it all.

"He always forgets shiitake mushrooms," Taro said to her. "I don't think he likes them. It's a psychological thing."

"You're a handsome couple," she said, feeling expansive.

She meant it. Taro's stark cheekbones, full lips, and tousled hair reminded her of her fantasies about the gardener this morning. She wondered if Taro's sweat would smell like Tony Lau's. Taro was dressed in that funky, effortless way Robert aspired to but was too stiff to carry off: black T-shirt, baggy jeans, bracelet of wooden beads around one wrist, glasses with rectangular frames. Robert, by comparison, tended to look like a slumming Brooks Brothers addict when he dressed down. Grace wondered if these two guys and Robert would get along or even have anything to say to each other.

Taro blushed. The woman in line behind him, even larger than Grace, spectacularly fat in the way Grace dreaded devolving into, with breasts hanging like limp missiles down either side of a submarine belly, scowled at them. Taro did not see this. He looked down at the items in his basket, then looked up again when his boyfriend returned. Grace looked down too – they had a slab of fish wrapped in brown paper, a bottle of good Pinot Noir, and various vegetables in plastic. Beyond the basket, on the same trajectory, her eyes couldn't escape the sight of the scowling woman's ankles, which flowed like candle wax over a pair of straining pumps.

Oh my God, I cannot let myself get to that point. Jesus help me. Buddha and Allah too, if you're listening.

Now it was time for Grace to choose paper or plastic. When she looked back, the two men were smiling at her and the woman behind them looked mere seconds away from a disdain-inspired aneurysm. Grace wished her all the luck and happiness she deserved.

I'm really going to do this.
I'm going to make it work.
I will not be stopped.

95

CHAPTER EIGHT:

ROBERT

Center of gravity. Cold wind at Baker Beach. Changing everything.

Clothes were not the problem any longer, Robert found. Gravity was. Growing up, he'd overheard obscure jokes between adults about how one's center of gravity tended to shift with age. Maybe that explained why so many grown men had paunches that cascaded over their belts like doomed scoops of ice cream seconds from plunging out of the cone. He'd heard of hernias but this sounded worse, and it became one of those simmering anxieties children grow up with but rarely mention, like the beginning of menses and the end of virginity. Now, with Robert's stomach a good fifteen pounds slimmer, he kept losing his balance. Even in earthquake-prone Northern California, he could only blame undulating floors for so long.

Stefan would know what to do.

Robert procrastinated before making the call. He made a mushroom omelet and a pot of coffee. As he chopped chanterelles (the recipe called for button mushrooms but they tasted like wet cardboard) and onions and half a bell pepper, he imagined Stefan probing the President's cranium for vestiges of a brain. How many Congressmen and corporate moguls didn't want to get old, or needed their diseases cured? Or would like to screw their mistresses and hookers again without pharmaceutical intervention? Stefan would be – in danger? No, that didn't make sense. He'd know how to take care of himself. He'd find a way to make himself rich, or richer. He'd be in incredible demand by the people who moved in those circles.

But he has already moved in those circles, an atavistic voice whispered. *If he wants something, all he has to do is make a phone call.*

Robert decided to add fresh basil to his omelet. And another egg, cholesterol be damned. What did it matter? He could eat pure lard if he wanted to. He could inject sugar into his own veins and drink corn syrup straight from the bottle. If he wanted chocolate cupcakes for breakfast every day for the rest of his life, he could have them.

You just have to know whom to call.

"Of course," Stefan said, when Robert worked up the nerve to phone him. "Muscle memory. I guess you are more finely tuned than I thought. You can never tell."

Of course. That explains everything. Robert thought of harps and pianos. He suspected Stefan meant *high-strung* or *tightly-wound*, even *uptight.* Robert wondered, *Am I uptight?* He couldn't tell. James would know. So would Grace, but if he were to ask, she might start sobbing, eat a gallon of Ben & Jerry's, and take a gun to the nearest outpost of 24 Hour Fitness to pick off fit people as they exited the gym. *I am not uptight. Hell, I'm not even as tight as I'd like to be.*

"Muscle memory?" Better bring himself back to the present. Robert didn't want to be one of those people who calls 911 because they've fallen down and they can't get up. And he'd like to keep Alzheimer's from setting in, if that could be arranged. The prospect of senility – real or imagined – horrified him.

"Yah, muscle memory. Your muscles remember, just like your brain. They get used to exerting a certain amount of force in a certain direction to accomplish different tasks, or make particular movements..."

"Right, I know what it is," Robert interrupted. In high school he'd only passed physics by copying off his friend Jason during tests. Stefan didn't need to know that. Unless he'd already found out while rummaging around in the toy box of Robert's brain. "So why am I walking into walls?"

"Because I didn't calibrate you correctly the last time," Stefan said. "I didn't compensate enough for a couple of factors."

Calibrate?

"Let me rephrase that," Stefan went on.

"Yeah, it feels funny to be talked about like a watch."

"You're more complicated than a watch," Stefan said. "Even a Rolex. You should know that. The body is a complex system. Even I don't know everything. Imagine you've lived in a big city like Los Angeles or Tokyo all your life. You grew up there, you went to school there, got married, raised the kids, and now you're in middle age. You know your city well, but do you know the name of every single street in the whole metropolis? Even if you've studied, do you know the color of every house on every block?"

"I think I see your point. Should I call a painter or buy a Thomas Guide?"

"No, just come back and let me work on you. I know what's wrong. I can fix it in twenty minutes, thirty if I see anything else that needs doing, and you'll be on your way."

Robert shifted on the sofa. Omelet finished, cup of double bergamot Earl Grey cooling on the coffee table, he stretched out. He didn't have to dread sleeping after a meal. He decided he'd be more comfortable lying in the opposite direction. Glare from the setting sun dazzled his eyes. Shade would be nice but he did like the ochre color of sunset on his walls. Comfort versus aesthetics – wasn't that the question pervading his entire life lately? Maybe he ought to ask Stefan to fix this irritating sensitivity to light – tweak those rods and cones, or tighten his irises.

"Sometimes I wonder…" Robert began.

"Yes?" The tiniest touch of impatience colored Stefan's voice. Or was it just a German thing? While living in Belgium, Robert had visited Berlin, Hamburg, Munich, Dresden, and several other cities. He skipped the Black Forest because after all the acid rain, who wants to see trees with psoriasis? He couldn't decide whether the Germans he met were all beer-swilling hicks in Mercedes or the most sophisticated people on earth. Perhaps both.

"Whether..." Fuck. Now he'd waded knee-deep into boiling waves. Might as well make soup of himself, he supposed. Pass the salt. "This is real. How can this be real? I mean, I see the difference every time I look in the mirror. My body is *different*. Better. I'm not complaining, but it's too much to take in all at once."

"Oh," Stefan said. "Of course it is. That's why we do it by degrees. To lessen the impact. And even at this rate, it's faster than you are prepared for. The body gains weight over time. Any abrupt change is disturbing, profoundly disturbing, even when the change is for the better. It will take time, Robert. But you'll be fine. You're healthier now than you ever have been, in all your life."

Robert fiddled with the fringe of his comforter. *Doona*, the Australians called them. Maybe he should quit his job and start a new life in Australia. Then he wouldn't have blankets and comforters in his linen closet, he'd have *doonas*. And he'd have a better accent. He could fade the pale remnants of his Carolina drawl into something more tart and antipodean. Sydney, in addition to looking like Vancouver and having Los Angeles weather, by all accounts teemed with gay men. Testosterone flowed in the gutters. Ultraviolet radiation from the bald spot in the ozone layer zapped everybody's hormones into overdrive. Go there, a well-traveled friend once told him, and indulge.

"It is overwhelming," Robert admitted. "I don't know how to take it all in. I want this to be true, and... you know. Lasting. I want it to last."

"Of course you do. What would be the point, otherwise?"

Stefan understood. Good. Robert wondered what face Stefan had been born with, whether Stefan had refined his art rearranging his own skin and bones before moving on to other people's. What would he otherwise look like today? Did he choose his present appearance – blandly, blondly handsome in a Visit Germany poster kind of way – to be unobtrusive? Not a blemish on him, no visible scars, nothing that would stand out? Robert suspected Stefan didn't want to be noticed... and stashed the question in the Things Not To Ask file along with half a million others.

"There's one other thing," Robert said. A red ribbon of fear tied itself around his stomach.

"Yes?"

Robert took a deep breath. "The cost," he said. "You've probably rooted around in my brain enough to know how much I earn. But what is this going to *cost?* Can I afford it?"

"Of course," Stefan said. He kept saying *of course* in that unctuous Teutonic accent which should have been reassuring but wasn't. "Do you think I'd see you if I thought the cost would be a problem?"

Robert hadn't thought about that aspect. He stared across the room at the three framed subway maps: London, Barcelona, and Milan. The colors of the lines all turned almost black in the sunset. London in particular held warm memories. He watched a short mental slide-show – memories of the ticket machines in Brixton, where he'd stayed, and Covent Garden, his first destination on the Tube.

"You worry yourself too much," Stefan said. "That's one of the greatest flaws of your culture, you Americans. You've all conditioned yourselves to doubt a good thing when it comes your way. The world isn't an evil place."

"I'm a lawyer," Robert said. "I need to question the good in everyone. If there's no ulterior motive, of what use is my job?"

"I don't know," Stefan said. "Maybe you need to think about that."

Robert stared at the ceiling, now an intriguing dark salmon color and deepening toward black. *I already think about it too much. I wake up every morning and "fuck" is the first word out of my mouth when I think about going to work. Another day, another ten, twelve, fourteen hours of drudgery. What's the point of life and liberty if there's no happiness to pursue?*

"I have some time this evening if you'd like to stumble over to my apartment," Stefan said. "Try not to trip and fall in front of a subway train, okay?"

"How does eight o'clock sound?" When Stefan said *fine*, Robert added, "I'll be there if my muscles can remember the way."

*

As a boy, Robert had never been fat. He swam on the municipal team for years. He ran cross country and set a few records. He had the appetite of a tyrannosaurus. A diet of scrambled eggs and sausage for most breakfasts, pizza for lunch, or maybe two sandwiches, and rivers of Gatorade only fuelled the fire. The bloodier the steak, the happier he felt about eating it. *You like 'em so rare they can still moo*, Gloria had once commented. *Better marry a Midwestern girl.* He stopped short of biting the heads off live fowl, *a la* Ozzy Osbourne, but at times he felt defined by his voracious need to *eat*. He'd been taut – hell, sometimes he jerked off to memories of his own naked body. The way he used to look: visible abs, smoothly curving pecs, grabbable biceps. This is the way he would look again. And God, let this not be some kind of extended hallucination. The real nightmare would be to wake up from a coma to find himself as flabby as ever, his new fitness only a delusion brought on by catastrophic brain damage. The second he recovered enough to walk, he'd jump off the Golden Gate Bridge. If he couldn't return to the coma-dream, might as well update his will and quit while he was ahead.

Stripping in front of the mirror was his new daily ritual. Between his morning two cups of coffee and his shower, he examined his body. Subtle changes pervaded. In the last few weeks, they'd all added up. Compounded, perhaps, like interest. He thought back to a recent conversation with Grace – *Don't hate your body, just hate individual parts of it. Today you can hate your thighs but you can't hate the whole package. Hate your ass tomorrow, and the day after that, you can hate the dingle-dangle where your triceps ought to be. It's a compromise, but it's not as bad as wallowing in self-disgust* – and cringed. His saliva tasted like aluminum foil. He wanted a couple of aspirin, not because he had a headache, but because he wanted to think about something other than what a *shit* he could be. (Well, she hadn't been to see Stefan. Whose fault was that, if not her own? At least he'd tried.)

Robert blamed law school for his obesity. When you're living and breathing the Socratic Method day in and day out, reading hundreds of pages of dense legalese until your eyes burn out like the picture tubes in antique TVs; when you're studying famous cases, writing briefs, and vying for a spot on the law review, there's neither time nor energy left for fitness. You go to seed. As an undergraduate, Robert kept up an exercise regimen. Once he hit law school, though, the pounds appeared out of thin air. Cheap empty-carb diets and sugary sodas kept him jittering well into the night, hours after his body demanded rest and entire regions of his mind slipped into an overworked paralysis. His eyes ached all the time from reading and his wrists ached half the time from typing. A low-grade headache lingered from six weeks into 1L until the end of his second year. Low-budget comestibles were his only readily available source of comfort; sex took too much time and effort.

Funny, he thought. *Now that I'm not horrified by my body, I have more perspective on it. Reality shifts. It's like a whole new law of physics. And I'm cheating this time around, too.*

"I hate my job." Robert clapped a hand over his mouth for a second, then realized what a silly, girlish gesture he'd just made. He looked at his hand as if it were false, or belonged to someone else.

He'd never said the words aloud before. Thought them, then chased them out of his head like Gloria chased out the neighbor's cat when it used to wander into their house. She'd grab a broom and run after the dull-witted tabby, screeching. The words sounded huge in the empty room. Other sounds bounced off them. Robert had once asked why didn't they just get a screen door and his mother answered, *Because we're Southern,* as if that explained anything. Now he looked around as if one of the senior partners might have materialized in his armchair, scowling.

"I hate my job. Oh my God, I hate my job."

He had to talk to James.

*

James answered his land line on the second ring. His cell phone dumped Robert into voice mail, and he only tried James's home number out of semi-desperation.

"I'm in mourning," he said, confirming a dark suspicion.

"What happened?" Robert kicked himself for wanting to ask *What else is new?* He resented whatever problem James might have. *I want to talk about me,* a terrible inner voice protested. *You're always miserable about something! I need you!*

"Bad enough that I drank two vodka tonics when I got home from work – and I left the office early."

"At?"

"Two."

Silence followed. Robert heard ice cubes clinking against glass.

"You're still drinking," he said.

"I know," James said. "When I poured the Stoli, I thought, *I'm still drinking*. Thanks for pointing it out, though."

"Why don't I come over?"

"Don't you want me to tell you what happened first? Before you rush to be by my side?"

Robert said, "Of course."

The doctor dumped James via e-mail, which James had printed out and was bitterly pleased to read over the phone: *This just isn't working for me. You're a nice guy but I don't think we're sexually compatible. I'm not sure who you are. I don't know how to talk about it. I'm sorry.*

"I thought I'd found someone good this time," James said.

You always think people are better than they are, Robert thought. But what he said was, "At least he didn't do it by sending a text message. E-mail's bad enough, but getting dumped by text would have been a disaster."

"It's a disaster anyway," James said.

Robert heard the clink of ice cubes at the bottom of an empty glass and wondered why cell phones picked up that kind of background noise but couldn't manage to transmit human voices with a reasonable degree of reliability. Half the time James sounded as if he were talking underwater and another quarter of the time static made the conversation impossible to follow.

"We always think they're good, at the beginning. Then they flake out. It's like some law of physics and we're helpless to do anything about it." Robert paused, aware his words weren't coming out quite right. "I'm so sorry," he said. "I'll be right over."

*

James wanted to go to the beach. Not just any beach, but Baker Beach, the clothing-optional one in San Francisco near the base of the Golden Gate Bridge. Robert would have been much happier with any of the other Bay Area beaches – Ocean Beach, Stinson Beach, even Santa Fucking Cruz. But James, sloshing with vodka, wanted to go to Baker Beach.

"You don't have to be nude," James said. "I want to be nude, but it's okay if you don't. You can wear a T-shirt and a bathing suit or whatever you want. You can wear a tarpaulin. But I want to be nude."

"You want to be nude," Robert said, as if he hadn't just heard the words two or three times. Next James would say he wanted to have oral sex with the President, the Secretary of State, and maybe the Pope. Robert kept thinking he'd got used to surprises, and he kept being surprised. Much more of this and his brain would feel the way a Jackson Pollack painting looks.

"I want to be nude." James nodded. "Stefan helped me like being nude. I have a nice body. It's not mine, but I like it anyway. I can pretend. I want to take off my clothes and lie in the sun. Everyone will look at me."

"You've always had a nice body," Robert said. "But the sun's setting. There aren't many rays left to catch."

"My dick was too small, and I didn't think the rest of me was... you know, proportional. All the biking made my quads too big, but my calves were skinny. My legs looked like drumsticks."

"Have you lost your mind?"

"No," James said. "I've found it. Look, you're going to have to drive. I'm too drunk."

"I have to see Stefan at eight," Robert said. "That won't leave us a lot of time."

"Then drop me off," James said. "Walk down to the beach with me, soak up the last of the sun, and go see Stefan. Come pick me up when you're done."

And that was how, half an hour later, Robert found himself in the parking lot that pretends it's the freeway approaching the Bay Bridge. Inching forward, wondering why in the name of hell people chose to live in a place where most of the day traffic doesn't move, he consoled himself: *I had to go into the City to see Stefan anyway. To be recalibrated. Because I'm uptight. How could anyone who does this commute not be uptight? Maybe Stefan can make me learn to love brake lights.*

By the time they reached the head of the trail leading down to the beach, Robert felt squeezed for time. You don't piss off the supernatural German who rearranges your entrails with his bare hands. Not if you don't want to be turned into bratwurst.

"I'll pick you up when we're done," Robert said.

James slumped in the passenger seat and looked miserable. He turned toward the window and rested his head against it.

Is he still seeing Stefan? Robert wondered. *But then, how could anyone stop?*

"You had it bad for that guy, didn't you?" he asked.

James nodded, and left a smudge of sebaceous oil on the glass.

Emotions warred in the lump of coal Robert called his heart. He felt sorry for James. He wanted to hold him and reassure him. He also felt giddy relief. With the doctor out of the picture, Robert wanted to crawl into bed next to James and comfort him and strip him naked...

"It's just 7," James said.

Robert heard him take a couple of deep breaths.

"Walk down the trail with me. If you leave at 7.30, you'll make it to Stefan's with time to spare."

"But parking," Robert protested.

"Park illegally," James said. "Everybody else does. I hope I'm more important to you than a fifty-dollar parking ticket."

*

Even this late in the day, with a cold breeze gusting in off the Pacific, the acres of naked flesh amazed Robert. Entire flocks of goosebumps migrated up and down his arms. His nipples stood at full attention. His penis wanted to hide. He followed James – who'd unselfconsciously shucked off his clothes halfway down the trail and tucked them in his backpack – in a state of turmoil, torn between not wanting to take his eyes off his friend's perfect tan buttocks and not wanting to miss any of the other men on display.

Not everyone's prone to shrinkage in a cold wind, he thought, eyeing the landscape. *Must be nice. I'll have to talk to Stefan about that too.*

Then he thought, *Why should I have to feel embarrassed about taking off my clothes? I've gone through the last decade barely able to stand the sight of myself. I've more than paid my dues. I've paid three or four other people's, too. Fuck it, I want a complete overhaul. Head to toe. Nothing left the same. I hate my job and every other aspect of my life and I really fucking hate the way I look. When Stefan's done with me, I don't want to recognize myself when I look in the mirror. That's what I want him to do. Change everything. Why not? I don't know who I am. Why not be somebody else?*

CHAPTER NINE:

GRACE

Photonegatives. Detritus of an eroding life. Personalized power grids.

Grace's cell phone emitted a tinny rendition of "Für Elise" from the depths of her purse. Manners dictated she let voice mail pick up, but Robert stopped talking and stared at her until she relented and answered the thing. When would she learn to switch off the ringer, to avoid moments like this?

"I'm on 101 near the airport, heading your way!" Flora Trust announced, after their customary greetings – exuberant (Flora Trust) and strained (Grace). Grace almost disconnected the call on the spot.

"You're what?" The news was bizarre and unpleasant. Worse, it might actually be true.

In the kitchen, somebody dropped what sounded like a dozen large metal pots and pans, then swore in Spanish. A wave of silence swept through the room. Conversations sparked back to life, tinged with amusement this time.

Robert made a face at something he saw in his plate of pasta. Grace still couldn't believe the sight of him. He could not have lost so much weight so soon without a tapeworm. She thought of her failure to catch volcanic dysentery on any of her trips to Mexico. Pangs of jealousy swirled like gin in the tonic of her annoyance at Flora Trust's call. And how dare Robert slim down on her like this? Three months ago he had more ass than a Bangkok boy-brothel. Goddamn it, he deserved a lingering case of the clap for abandoning her. He deserved to keep shrinking until he looked like a photonegative of himself. He glared at his pasta while she looked helplessly around the café, cell phone pressed against her head to drown out background noise, Flora Trust's pile-driver of a voice hammering into her left ear. Grace winced with every syllable.

"I just passed SFO! I drove down from Oregon for the weekend! You wouldn't believe what time I started driving this morning!"

"Holy fuck," Grace said.

"Wash your mouth out with soap!" Flora Trust exclaimed.

Grace eyed her Caesar salad. The strips of grilled chicken breast atop glistening layers of lettuce leaves did not appeal to her in the least. *This is your life now,* she told herself. She'd been especially good today and foregone the grated parmesan cheese in favor of ground pepper and a few squirts of juice from a lemon wedge. Robert, on the other hand, had ordered a decadent mound of seafood pasta. The baby squid frightened Grace. She didn't want to eat tentacles or anything else that looked capable of movement. If Robert wanted to, she was fine with that, but then, she imagined he put all kinds of nasty things in his mouth. Bits of squid paled in comparison to unwashed foreskin and the soles of boots.

Her air-raid siren of a sister kept bellowing: "I signed us up for the workshop! I figured I hadn't seen you in a coon's age, so I just hopped in the car and drove right down!"

"What workshop?"

Robert picked up something between his thumb and forefinger. Grace couldn't tell what it was. He examined it like a jeweler with a suspect diamond. She took a sip of white wine (her one indulgence for the day) and mentally steadied herself for whatever bombshell would next come hurtling out of Flora Trust's mouth.

"The women's empowerment one? Personalized power grids?"

"Flora Trust, you know how I feel about empowered women with grids."

"Dorothy Grace, I know how you feel about a lot of things, and that doesn't mean you're not so full of shit that it's oozing out of your pores. I signed us up for the workshop, and it's tomorrow morning, and whatever plans you have, you're going to cancel them. I have spoken."

Grace drained her glass. Robert had gone pale around the edges, as if he'd seen the seafood in his linguine moving. Served him right.

How did you do this? So much weight – I can't believe it, she'd said when they met on the sidewalk outside the café.

It's this guy I told you about, Stefan. He really puts you on a program.

A program? Like Windows? How often does it crash? How virus-prone is it?

You've been living in Silicon Valley too long, Grace.

"But Rich is going to be home all weekend," Grace said. As she spoke, she felt her resolve eroding. When Flora Trust got on a roll, resistance was futile. Grace felt herself being assimilated. "I was thinking about maybe spending some time with him…"

Robert spoke up: "Bullshit. He'll call you and tell you he has to work all day Saturday, plus Sunday morning, and then he'll come home, take a shower, and pass out cold in front of the TV. You'll have to listen to football games all afternoon."

The tide of this conversation whisked Grace out to sea. She struggled not to drown.

"Just tell me where to meet you," Flora Trust said. "I'm getting close to the exit. Damn, girl, traffic sucks here! How do you stand it?"

"I don't," Grace said. "I try to avoid the freeways."

"Like you try to avoid reality."

Grace chose not to respond. Flora Trust was better at this than she was. Grace resigned herself to a weekend of feeling twelve again, and told her sister the name of the café. Even if Robert had to leave, she could still wait. It wasn't as if she had anywhere to go or anything pressing to do. The beauty of most of her errands was their utter lack of necessity. Perhaps another wine spritzer would be just the thing. It would brace her up and smooth out the rough edges before her sister's visit.

Grace thought, *Power grids and twat astronomy. I definitely need more wine.*

Half an hour later, after Robert had excused himself, Flora Trust swooped in. Every head in the diner turned.

Grace thought, *Let the braying begin.*

*

"What's all this no-carb bullshit in your refrigerator?" Flora Trust asked, after dumping two faded, shapeless overnight bags (so covered with cat hair they'd purr if you stroked them) in the guest bedroom. In the kitchen, Flora Trust opened a cupboard and whooped laughter when she saw the organic cereal, diet bars, and pouches of dried fruit. "Holy shit, girl, you're serious! What's up?"

Grace thought of the way Rich had looked at her this morning, on his way out of the house. True, he was in more of a hurry than usual. Early meeting, gotta prepare, blah blah blah. She told him to have a nice day and he'd responded with the slightest pause in his step, then that trademark tight smile that meant *It's over.* A black tide of grief had been surging through her all day. She wanted a life preserver. She wanted Valium. She wanted vodka. She wanted an entire bag of Doritos, a bottle of Vanilla Pepsi, a dozen Krispy Kreme donuts, and about half a pound of dark chocolate. Anything but this screaming emptiness.

"I'm trying to lose a little weight," Grace said.

"You've been trying to lose a little weight for years," Flora Trust said. "Crumbling two Atkins Bars your quart of Ben & Jerry's isn't going to do it, honey. Listen to your sister. You're a *woman*, not a picture in a magazine. You're beautiful just like you are, and screw Rich if he can't see that!"

"Just like that?" Grace asked. She wanted to be vulnerable for a minute, then remembered it's impossible to snuggle up with a wrecking ball. "I'm doing it for my health. It's not about Rich."

The dark tide flooded back in. She looked around her kitchen at the plastic bags of dried fruit, the dozen yellow tulips beginning to wilt in their Crate & Barrel vase, the wine glasses drying in the dish rack by the sink. Even the pewter knobs on the drawers and cabinets depressed her today: detritus from an eroding life.

Flora Trust opened the refrigerator again and looked inside, presumably to see whether new, less wholesome food had appeared. Grace heard her take a deep breath and let it out slowly.

"You want Rich back. You're miserable. It's all over your face. Don't think you're not an open book, Grace."

"I hope I'm well-written," Grace said.

"Don't get started," Flora Trust said. "Is Rich going to be home tonight?"

Grace shook her head. "Well," she amended. "He might be. There's no telling. He might be screwing one of the paralegals tonight, or he might be screwing someone else I don't know about yet, or he might legitimately be working late, or he might just not feel like coming home to look at my fat ass. I never know from one day to the next."

"And this is a relationship you think you want to hold onto?"

"You know an alternative?"

"A good vibrator. Best investment a girl can make. I've got this little one, about the size of my palm, and it has three speeds…"

"I hired a detective," Grace said, cutting off Flora Trust's paean to sex toys and generally trying to sound braver than she felt.

"Are you fucking him?"

"No!"

"But you're blushing. It's crossed your mind. Perhaps you should be. What do you need a detective for, anyway, if you're not fucking him?"

"Documenting Rich's… I don't know what word to use. Transgressions." Grace's hands were shaking now. Ironic that she lived with a lawyer but never felt cross-examined until her sister came to visit. This would be a great time for another glass of wine, she decided. Fuck the diet. She'd go to the gym tomorrow morning before Flora Trust dragged her to the Women's Wail-In or whatever it was called.

"What on earth for? You're planning to divorce him? Good for you!" Flora Trust leaned against the counter and fiddled with a paper towel from the roll. She'd torn it off and crumpled it up, apparently to give herself something to play with. A recovering smoker, Flora Trust had to keep her fingers busy.

"No, I'm planning to keep him." This conversation could not end soon enough. Grace felt no desire whatsoever to discuss plans with her sister. "You must be exhausted from the drive down. Why don't you take a nap? I think I'd like one, myself."

"Nah, I'll be fine. Just brew a pot of coffee. We'll sit around and catch up!"

Given the choice between more catching up and being force-fed a thousand live crickets, Grace would have happily tied on a bib and asked for the bugs.

"I'm feeling sleepy after my lunch. If you want coffee, I'll brew you a pot, but I really have to lie down and shut my eyes for a little while."

"Dorothy Grace, as I live and breathe," Flora Trust said. "When did you turn into our grandmother?"

*

The day stretched out like a prison term when Grace saw the workshop's registration materials. She couldn't decide whether the presenters' bios disturbed her or amused her: *Belinda Wolfwomon, BA/CI/CT, is a womon-identified dyke feminist from Ocala, Florida. A born communicator, she has had a varied, rich, and rewarding career combining a number of diverse aspects: sign language interpreter, peer counselor, performer, personal life skills coach, reiki instructor, and change catalyst. She has published articles and personal essays in womyn's magazines and journals, and is now currently working on her novel-in-progress, SISTERS UNDER THE MOON, which she hopes to self-publish via eBooksRUs.com. She invites you to challenge yourself, reach for new horizons, expand your awareness on all levels, and be the most powerful womon you can be.*

"Oestrogen poisoning," Grace said under her breath. She felt a little [sic], and decided not to read the other womon's bio – Nananne something-hyphenated-or-other. What on earth would their mothers think?

"What did you say about boysenberries?" Flora Trust asked. "The rest of the boysenberries?"

"Boysenberries? Oh, right, I'm out of them. Let's stop at the store on the way home," Grace said. "I want to bake a pie."

"That's so domesticated of you!" chirped the magenta-haired womon at the registration desk. Reading glasses on a chain rappelled off the sheer cliffs of her bosom.

Grace's mouth opened but no words came out.

"Oh, she's quite domesticated," Flora Trust said. "You have no idea. And you know what's best? We have a litter box set up for her at home for her to pee in. We didn't bring the leash, though. She does really well without it. Today's special so we didn't even bring the collar. We have a relationship built on trust. Honey, are you coming? I don't want to miss a single thing!" To the registration woman, whose face now matched her hair, Flora Trust waved and smiled. "Bye now!"

Flora Trust guided Grace (who was trying not to giggle) by the arm to an empty pair of chairs. She had just enough time to think *Fuck, and I have to sit in a folding metal torture rack all day on top of everything else* before her sister strong-armed her into a seated position.

"That was the most disgusting thing I've ever heard!" Grace hissed. "Jesus Christ, Flora Trust, what got into you? Where did you learn to talk like that?"

"What are you complaining about? I just rescued you from Crayola-head's clutches."

"Oh, I'm not complaining one bit, it was brilliant, but... what go into you?"

"That stupid cunt calling you domesticated, that's what got into me."

A couple of the knots of tension in Grace's chest uncoiled.

"Don't you think I'm domesticated too?" she asked, breathing easier now.

"You want to be," Flora Trust said. "Desperately, I'd say. But you're not. I don't know why you won't let go and just be who you are. I mean, look at yourself. You're married to an unfaithful man, you're driving yourself nuts trying to hold onto him, and I don't think you really know what you want, but it's not for me to say. I just couldn't have her talking to you in that patronizing tone of voice. That shit just gripes my ass, honey. You have no idea."

"Why not? I thought... radical empowered femi-nazis of a feather stick together. I don't know."

"You're my sister," Flora Trust said. "Fuck that pink-haired cunt and her *my pussy tastes better than yours* bullshit."

Grace took a series of deep breaths and let the golden shower of surrealism wash over her.

*

Highlights of the day, in no particular order:

One: The famed and fabled Power Grids. Nananne passed out 8½ x 11 sheets of pastel pink paper onto which a maze of intersecting lines and curves had been photocopied. *It looks like a natal chart*, Flora Trust whispered, and Grace nodded, although she had no idea what a natal chart was, nor why she should care. Nananne spouted instructions that grew less comprehensible with each passing second. Other women nodded and filled in information – need for affection (on a scale from 1 to 10), intensity of orgasms with your regular partner (on a scale of 1 to 5), intensity of orgasms while masturbating (also on a scale of 1 to 5), average number of other-centered choices made per day (whatever *other-centered choices* were, Grace didn't know and didn't want to ask; on a scale of 1 to 20), personal stress level (on a scale of 1 to 50), and so on. Grace expected the UFOs to land at any moment. Bring on the anal probes. She gave up listening, took a few colored markers out of her purse, and colored squares until Belinda caught her and said *I think you would really benefit from this activity if you would give Nananne your undivided attention, and perhaps really give some thought to your disempowerment as a womon, because you are dismissing this exercise.* Grace wished she could fart on command.

Two: Personal Sharing. Or, the sob-fest Grace had been dreading.

These women didn't run with the moon or even howl at it, apparently, because they were too busy bawling about abstract concepts like oppression and the patriarchy. For a single second, when her turn came, her throat constricted. She didn't want to talk about Rich. It was nobody's goddamn business, particularly not these two nosy Gaia-worshipping snatches who were doubtless so busy eating each other out in their spare time they'd forgotten that some women still marry men and want to hang onto them. *I'm here about my...* Grace began. She made her chin quiver, and summoned more crocodile tears. She sank into her chair and wept on her sister's shoulder until the spotlight was directed at someone else. Nananne said, *Just think about the learning that you've taken away from this, Grace, and what that learning is trying to tell you. It's telling you to be in integrity. Just be. You can make things better for yourself, but you have to arrive at a space where you can embrace the betterness.* Grace closed her eyes and thought how much better life in America would be with an English-language equivalent to the Académie Française.

Three: Body-centered movement exercises. Belinda strode round the room, leading a group of women in a loose conga line. *It's important to realize that you shape your circumstances just by the way you hold your body. Your posture determines everything. Every perception people have. Even your self-concept.* Grace thought of Gloria and her talk of finishing school. *It didn't take,* Gloria had once said. *I may be able to walk across the room with a book balanced on top of my head, but look how I turned out!* Look indeed. Grace watched Belinda and the dozen or so (out of about 50, and where did they all come from?) women following her. Belinda called, *Lead with your forehead!* A dozen heads nodded forward. Grace couldn't see a difference. *Lead with your chest!* Two dozen breasts jutted outward. Grace still couldn't see a difference. How was this prancing supposed to shape an interaction, unless you were trying to blind someone with your nipples? *Lead with your stom-*

ach! A dozen tummies strained as the conga line circled the room. Grace tuned them all out and fiddled with her cuticles until she heard the words *Lead with your anal cavity!* At which point she got up and left the room.

CHAPTER TEN:

ROBERT

Godzilla's wife and Schrödinger's cat. Kagoshima. Airborne sheep.

Flora Trust was, in Robert's estimation, a big frightening wind-up doll that walked and talked and knocked things down. He preferred to avoid her, family ties be damned. She'd have made Godzilla a good wife if she'd been the marrying type and he'd been something other than a special effect. When Flora Trust called Grace and said she'd be arriving soon, Robert made his excuses and fled for his life. He didn't want to answer her bullhorn-loud questions about his weight loss and whether he'd had lipo. Nor did he want to subject the innocent bystanders dining in the café to her noise pollution.

He opened the refrigerator a second time, knowing no new food had appeared since the last time he'd looked. He'd used the last of the eggs in yesterday's omelet. Condiments, vegetation of dubious freshness, and one slice of bread (not counting the crust at the end of the loaf, which he refused to eat on general principle) could not be combined to make anything resembling a meal. Even calling them food stretched the definition of the term. Maybe the contents of refrigerators disappeared and reappeared the way Schrödinger's hypothetical cat lived and died: when he closed the door, luscious drinks and snacks reappeared; when he opened it again, they vanished. The fridge was always empty and full simultaneously. Everything depended on timing. If he could just open the door fast enough, at the right moment, he'd never need to go to Trader Joe's.

Robert had been conducting an experiment to see how much junk food he could eat without gaining weight. After two days of Enormo-Sizing his McGarbage and washing his Crapburgers down with gallons of Diet Sludge, he gave up. Weight or no weight, he couldn't stand the salt, sugar, and grease. He couldn't decide which smelled worse, the pseudofood itself or the cardboard containers he discarded after eating. French fries gave off a toxic miasma as they decomposed. Shreds of lettuce swimming in rancid sauce smelled even worse. He'd have to make a grocery store run before he grossed himself the rest of the way out.

"There's nothing quite like having nothing in the house..." He half-spoke and half-sang the words, idly wondering if anyone had ever used them in a pop song.

In the cupboard, he found two types of dry pasta (fusilli and capellini), but no sauce and not even enough olive oil to sauté a couple of garlic cloves. He found a bag of tortilla chip debris – fragments of two different brands, possibly three. (He ate the unbroken chips with salsa verde and poured the remains into the next bag he bought. Eventually he would end up with an entire bag of crunchy shrapnel, which he supposed he would have to eat sooner or later.) In addition to the earthly remains of the bell pepper, the vegetable crisper contained fraying broccoli and an onion whose outer layers were peeling like sunburned skin. Two potatoes had sprouted, then given up on life. The freezer contained empty ice cube trays, one popsicle (purple, the only color he disliked), and a bag of frozen chicken breasts. Someone with culinary talent could turn these odds and ends into a meal; Robert decided the best solution was to dump everything but the chicken breasts into the garbage can, as he had done with his bathroom products.

Growing up, he'd looked forward to Gloria's "throw it all out" dinners.

When she couldn't be bothered to cook, she pulled out all the odds and ends in the fridge and the pantry, spread it all out on the table, and called it a meal. Cold cuts, canned pineapple chunks conveniently speared with colorful toothpicks, peanuts, fruit juice, whatever vegetables she happened to have on hand, slices of apple. She'd scramble eggs with shredded sandwich ham. One time she tried frying rice but produced something the consistency of old dog food. Happy memories, useless today.

Grace had spoken of legendary grocery store raids. She sacked supermarkets like the Spartans sacked Troy. The employees at Whole Foods cheered when they saw her coming because she was singlehandedly putting some of their kids through college, or at least paying for new tattoos and facial piercings. He could ask nothing less of himself, especially now that he was immune to calories.

*

Any minute now, James would call. He couldn't not call. Robert had left a tantalizing voice mail message for him: *Hi James, you're not going to believe this but this is the third day I've called out sick. Parsons took me aside and said he's concerned about the way I look. People are talking about it. So I should just take some time and focus on getting well. Can you believe that shit? He even offered to refer me to a specialist at the Mayo Clinic. I told him I was fine but he didn't believe me. And apparently there are all kinds of rumors going around about me. They think I've either got cancer or AIDS. Look, I think you should blow work off too. We'll go back to the beach. I'll even take my clothes off this time. You're taking this thing with the doctor hard, and I want to be there for you. Call me back when you get this. If you're moping again, stop at once.*

Robert paced. He had groceries to buy, laundry to drop off at and pick up from the dry cleaners, videos to return, and several other errands to run.

His car, the same Subaru Legacy he'd been driving since law school, would thank him for an oil change if it could talk. He needed to pay a few bills online. What must it be like, he wondered, to live without these needling obligations? Even the über-rich had worries, he presumed: they needed to keep an eye on their mountains of money. (The rest of life's chores could be delegated.) He stood at the window and looked out, not at the Oakland Hills but at the middle distance beyond them. When had he last watered his plants? The cacti looked happy but the spider plant looked as if he'd baked it. His orchids had changed their minds about blooming: yellow and purple buds littered the tabletop.

So many things to do; so few things he would actually enjoy doing.

The idea *A few more sessions with Stefan, and James will finally want me* struck Robert like a moderate earthquake. Fault lines rumbled in his brain; thoughts tumbled off his mental bookshelves. *Who am I doing this for? Myself, or James? Or am I doing it because to be a metrosexual American male, or just a fag, or whatever the hell we're supposed to call ourselves these days, this is what you're supposed to look like? Having the same figure as a matronly walrus is Not Allowed?*

What if James didn't want him?

I have too much time on my hands, Robert thought. *I wouldn't be so haunted if I were busy at the office.*

He'd had crushes before. They ended in coldness or tears. In his last year of high school, he couldn't stop thinking about his best friend Scott, a depressed half-Japanese guy whose mother kept trying and failing to commit suicide. She overdosed on pills and threw them all up on the living room carpet before passing out in a pool of her own vomit. Scott had been the one to find her. Two weeks later she'd cut both wrists with an X-acto knife but hadn't cut deep enough. The blood made a terrible mess in the bathroom. The house went on the market; the family moved across town.

Scott talked less and less. He lost weight (not that he had much to spare) and looked pale most of the time. He said his father wanted him to go live with his grandparents in Kagoshima. Robert convinced himself that if they were together, Scott would be happier. He wouldn't be so depressed if he had a boyfriend who adored him. In theory, that's how it would have worked. In practice, Scott moved to Japan without saying goodbye. Robert called and Scott's mother hung up on him. An apologetic letter came a month later: *I knew you wanted to be closer but there wasn't anything inside me to get close to. I don't know if I like guys or not and maybe someday I'll figure it out. The volcano here is called Sakurajima, and it's always raining ash over the city. You always know you're living on the brink. The kids here call me gaijin, but I'm only half white. I can speak Japanese. I don't get it. Some days I think it would be easier to hike up to the top of the volcano and jump in.*

The warble of Robert's cell phone interrupted his obsession session.

"Oh!" he exclaimed, running to grab the phone before voice mail picked up. Sweat slicked his fingers. He dropped the thing, caught it in midair, and fumbled to flip it open. "James! You got my message! I'm off work again today, and Stefan worked another miracle and we have *got* to go to the beach!"

A silver nail of silence pricked Robert's ear.

"Grace?" he asked.

"Any minute now, you're going to tell me why you're not at work," she said.

"Parsons told me to hang out at home for a few days because people are talking. Parsons says they're *concerned*. Whatever *concerned* means. Look, let's be realistic, Rich is going to make partner, and I'm not, so what difference does it make?" There. He'd said it out loud. Grace squawked, but Robert kept talking: "I'm not sure when I figured it out, but I did, and you know, I just can't be bothered this week."

123

Another prickly silence, punctuated by erratic breathing. Robert paced in his living room, where he got the best reception. The midmorning sun made squares of yellow light on the carpet. He needed to vacuum. Further drudgery to avoid if possible. The bare stems of his orchids disturbed him. He tried walking into the kitchen to get them out of his sight, but a burst of static put an end to that idea. Typical Bay Area scenario: his cell phone only worked in one room of his home. Could Stefan work on whatever misfiring synapses led Robert to dislike housework? Probably not. Stefan would say something obscure like *The mind/body divide is arbitrary* and change the subject. Besides, he didn't invest much time in housekeeping, himself. His supernatural talents apparently did not extend themselves to dusting and picking up the ATM receipts and movie ticket stubs that littered his coffee table and the top of his TV.

"Grace?"

"What?"

"Is everything okay? You're not pissed off at me now, are you? I'm sorry. I shouldn't have been that blunt with you."

"Of course you should be blunt with me," Grace said. "I'm your sister. Who else are you going to be blunt with? James? Oh wait – no, the part about wanting to pick out matching tuxes for the wedding would scare him off. He'd check himself into Napa and you'd never see him again. Guess that leaves me."

"Twat," Robert said.

"I'm going nuts," Grace said.

"Going?"

Under normal circumstances she'd have insulted him back. Maybe she'd been damaged by that women's empowerment workshop.

"Why is that?"

"I should get off the phone. James might call. I know he's the one you really want to talk to."

"Chill out. I've got call waiting. What's going on? You sound confused. Are you sick?"

"I'm dieting," she said. "I'm going to get my husband back, remember?"

Dieting, Jesus. Robert had been down that road. Salads. Cold water with a slice of lemon. Lots of green tea because it was supposed to be slimming. Boneless, skinless chicken breasts – microwaved, and sprinkled with a pinch of garlic salt and black pepper. A single low-carb nutrition bar for breakfast when he couldn't be bothered to wash an apple or peel himself an orange. He'd fully explored the lower depths of diet hell, decided he could only burn for so long, and gone on to commit multiple mortal caloric sins. Sometimes after starving himself for a couple of weeks he even craved cigarettes, just for the rebellious thrill of mistreating his body. He wanted to drink cheap scotch straight from the bottle, with fluorescent blue Gatorade as a chaser. Until now, the prospect of losing a noticeable amount of weight seemed fatuous. It was like winning the lottery: it happened to other people, but had many of the same qualities as an urban myth.

"Grace, you're not going to slim down by not eating. You'll gain it all back later, and then some, and you'll still be miserable. Trust me, I've been down that road and so have you."

"Oh, I'm eating," she said. "But I'm not used to, you know, eating less. I feel funny. My head… it goes all swimmy. It's like my brain would fall out if it weren't encased in something. My skull. It's the only thing holding my brain in."

"Then you should eat something."

"No, I should fix another cup of green tea. That helps. Lots of green tea." Inwardly, Robert groaned. Grace babbled on: "I bought like five different kinds at the store. Maybe six? I didn't count them. Who would have imagined there were so many different kinds of green tea? There's Tazo

125

and Stash and Celestial Seasonings, and this organic kind called Choice, and they make this Earl Grey with lavender too..."

"Grace, honey, what are you on?"

"Buddhist monks have something called tea mind," Grace jabbered. "They drink tea and meditate all day, and they're *skinny*! That's what I'm trying for. Tea mind. I want to be skinny so I can fit into jeans from the Gap."

"Tea mind? You mean, *tea ass*. Grace, go eat something. I don't know what tea mind is, and I don't think I care. I do think a ham sandwich would be healthier right now. Go fix yourself a ham sandwich. A big huge one. Put butter on the bread. Big hunks of cheese. Drink some fruit juice. It'll raise your blood sugar faster."

"No," she said. "I'm serious about this, Robert. I have to win Rich back, and this is the only way."

By driving yourself nuts?

Grace named a new herbal weight-loss supplement. Robert hadn't heard of it, but it couldn't be any different from the other ones.

"I thought I'd try these. They're new. They were developed in Switzerland," Grace said.

"Oh, that makes them special," Robert said.

"I'm serious, they're organic and they have botanical essences. The Swiss are good at things like that. Bank accounts, too. The Swiss are good at bank accounts and botanical essences."

"They used to be good at running airlines, too," Robert said.

Grace gave no sign she'd even heard him. "There's no ephedra, and not so much caffeine. It's mostly – here, let me read the label: taurine, maté, guaraná, and gotu kola."

"And herbal essences. Flush the essences down the toilet," Robert said. Gotu kola? Sounded like a junk-food oriented board game for fat third-graders. Gotu ice cream. Gotu pepperoni pizza. Or a command. Do not pass Go. Do not collect $200. Gotu kola.

A barbed-wire strand of nausea twisted in his guts at the thought of Grace strung out on diet pills. He'd been there. In fact, he'd traveled the length and breadth of that country so often that he'd worn out his passport. He'd seen all the tourist sites, sampled the local cuisine, and not lost an ounce that hadn't come back threefold. Grace hadn't gone to see Stefan. If she kept this up, she'd need to be delivered to his apartment on a stretcher. She was out of her mind. She needed an intervention but you couldn't call 911 for things like this, Flora Trust was back in Oregon (and frightening), and Rich couldn't be bothered.

"I can't." Grace sounded distracted. Robert imagined she was staring out the window, counting clouds. With all that taurine, maté, guaraná, and gotu kola coursing through her veins, the clouds in the sky probably went *baaa* like so many head of sheep. "I spent so much on them. And they really work."

"How do you know? Because they're from Switzerland? Because the infomercial said so? Grace, you know better than this. We used to laugh at the Psychic Friends Network. Tell me you're going to get off those things. Don't take any more of them. Promise me."

"I promise," she said.

Robert heard the lie in her voice but before he could call her on it, she said she had to go and hung up on him.

What is it about me that makes people do that? Why doesn't anyone bother saying goodbye? What on earth was I like in my former life?

He thought on this for a moment, pushed thoughts of strange karma out of his head, then called Grace back.

"Promise me you'll flush the pills, and I'll take you to a spa this weekend. I heard about one up in the Sierra; we should check it out. We'll drive

127

up, buy some wine, get herbal mud massages and hot stone treatments and whatever else our black little hearts desire. Okay? *Just flush the goddamn pills, Grace."*

This time, when she said she would, he almost believed her.

Next, Robert contemplated calling Rich at work, then decided not to. What would it accomplish? What was there to say? *So, Rich, about your wife. You remember her, right? That woman you married and used to sleep with? My sister? A little on the heavy side, but pretty? Right, yeah, her. Look, you know, she's strung out on some kind of herbal speed because she's trying to lose weight, to hold onto your worthless ass, and maybe if you'd give some thought to, I don't know, speaking to her? Maybe not quite so openly fucking every other woman within a half-mile radius? She might be a lot healthier. Just a thought. And go home now, because she needs you. If she has kidney failure or some kind of stroke from overdosing on that shit, I'm going to reach up your ass, pull out your heart, and feed it to you.*

He couldn't really say that. Rich would piss himself laughing, so Robert contented himself to think it.

*

At odds with himself, he called James again. He had to bleed off this nervous energy. If he were to lay on his sofa a minute longer, watching the squares of sunlight move across the carpet (which he still hadn't vacuumed), he'd go nuts. More nuts. Organic filberts from Switzerland nuts, with pure Alpine botanical essences. Any second now the clouds would turn into sheep and swoop through his open window and say *You need to vacuum.* When had he last vacuumed, anyway? What about dusting? Why wasn't James answering his phone? Had he looked in the mirror, seen perfection, and flung himself off a parapet in gorgeous despair?

Maybe I should go to the office after all? Do some work?

Even if he stood at best a snowball's chance in hell of making partner, and was losing his ability to care, he had bills to pay.

Sooner or later Stefan would send him an invoice, too.

Robert wondered whether he'd be able to afford it.

He ran his hands up and down his newly-flat stomach.

You're doing the right thing, he reassured himself.

He promised himself he'd find a way, regardless of the cost. He had come this far, hadn't he? Plus, he'd turned in his fat-boy passport at the border. Having renounced his citizenship, he could neither turn back nor imagine why he would want to.

CHAPTER ELEVEN:
GRACE

Swedish engineering. A whole day of beauty. Toxins.

The drive to Oakland from Palo Alto took less time than Grace had expected, even at 80 miles per hour early on a Saturday morning: neither traffic nor the California Highway Patrol impeded her progress. The air above the Oakland Airport, an alarming shade of tan the last time she'd driven this route, all but sparkled. As she sped north, she saw two planes take off and two others land. The words *a certain slant of flight* left distracting thought-contrails inside her mind. For a second she wished she were on her way to the airport, about to travel again. Then she recalled the slow asphyxiation of waiting for Rich in Paris.

What's this "waiting for" bullshit, Grace? You were stalking him, Gloria said. *You're too old to play pretend about things like that.*

Grace floored the accelerator and pushed the Volvo up to 85, 90, 95, and cranked up the volume on the stereo to drown out both her angst and her mother.

Her last visit to Robert's apartment had been a disaster of timing: like an idiot, she'd left her house on the Peninsula at 3.00 PM. Traffic on the Dumbarton Bridge (nicknamed Dumbo by the locals), which crossed the southern half of the Bay, flowed like old glass from a windowpane. I-880 northbound was equally deathsome; she wondered what her speed equaled in inches per hour. Her head pounded. Aneurysms threatened. *At this rate I'll be dead before I reach Robert's place*, she remembered thinking. Grace's knee and ankle ached from the back-and-forth action of braking and tentative acceleration. Nothing a Valium and a few Demerol wouldn't fix, but she hadn't brought a bottle of water along, and those pills were about as easy to dry-swallow as children's building blocks.

Lost in horrendous nostalgia, and enrapt by the angle of an Alaska Airlines jet ascending, she missed Robert's exit and got lost in the Macarthur Maze, the labyrinth of elevated flyovers and interchanges that nobody, even locals, successfully navigates every time. *Who's responsible for this mess*, she had once asked Rich, not long after their arrival in California. He replied, *The same engineers who designed hell, I imagine.* Now Grace found herself on Highway 24 speeding east toward Outer Suburbia, squinting into the glare of the morning sky. She recognized a last-chance Oakland exit and swerved across two mercifully empty lanes to make the ramp.

"Swedish engineering," she said. Her heart roared like the Volvo's engine. She tended to be a sedate driver but with a screaming case of starvation-induced jitters, she scared herself behind the wheel. Fortunately the car could compensate for her nervous shortcomings. Grace basked in a moment of love for her sedan. It seemed to love her back.

At least somebody did.

*

"You look thinner," were Robert's first words, when he opened his door after her knock. She'd been expecting to hear *You look like a pregnant manatee this morning*. Now and then he surprised her. He hadn't lost his touch. Besides, she was so sore and frazzled after pounding herself to a pulp at the gym all week, fuelled by diet Red Bull, near-starvation, and crying fits, she'd have jammed her thumbs into his eyes without hesitation if any words other than *You're thinner* had come out of his mouth.

"I do?" A spark of contentment glowed in her soul. Or maybe it was just gastric reflux from skipping dinner last night. "Really? I've lost seven pounds this week. Does it show?"

Robert nodded.

"You're looking relatively skeletal, yourself," Grace said.

Actually, at this rate he'd be antimatter soon, and the universe would implode around him. No wonder he was calling out sick all the goddamn time. Even if he didn't have something fast and fatal like pancreatic cancer, he couldn't show his face at the office without starting a riot. Everyone who didn't think he was dying would call him the Messiah and beg him to share some of the miracle. He could have his own talk show. He'd eat Oprah for lunch and Ellen for dinner and not need a doggie bag for the leftovers.

"You don't mind driving, do you?" Grace asked, after a trip to the bathroom to make sure her eyes weren't too red. They weren't. She applied a few drops of Visine to keep them that way. "I'm feeling a little bit off this morning."

"I was going to suggest it."

*

"Rich is leaving for Paris again on Monday," Grace said

Robert swerved to avoid something black in the road: scraps from a blown-out tire, she supposed. Grace instinctively tightened her grip on the Oh-Jesus bar, and her toes curled. She questioned her decision to let him drive her car, then wished she'd driven Rich's Lancia and encouraged Robert to wreck it. *Why don't I get out while you wrap this thing around a tree? I promise you won't get hurt much if you ram into something on the passenger's side. You can pretend you're in a JG Ballard novel. And I'll give you twenty grand?* There had to be something wrong with him: some disease, maybe a parasite or a pill habit. She thought of asking, *How long is your tapeworm?* (The envious fat girl's equivalent to *What color is your parachute?*) The shadow of guilt that darkened his face made him look as haggard as she felt.

"I knew about that trip," he said. "Don't tell me you didn't?"

Grace turned to look at him. He needed to shave. She couldn't read his expression well in profile, but his eyes widened. He was staring straight ahead, the cords in his neck rigid, as if he were in the electric chair instead of the driver's seat.

His double chin is gone, too. Motherfucker. Mine needs its own bra.

"I've seen him for a total of two hours in the last week. More if you count the time he was asleep."

"He didn't e-mail you or leave a note? Nothing?"

"You're asking me like you don't already know the answer."

Robert drove in silence a few minutes before commenting. She looked at his hands: less meaty. He needed a manicure. She had misgivings about men who got manicures – it didn't seem masculine – but fraying cuticles were every bit as appalling. When did he start wearing a silver ring on each middle finger? Why hadn't she noticed before?

"Not even a phone call?" Robert asked.

Grace wanted to ask him to stop the car at the next gas station. No restaurant would be open this early, not this far out in the Wine Country. The resort, nestled in the foothills of the Sierra, was at least two hours away. If she didn't eat something soon, she'd be forced to rip strips of leather off the seat backs. She wanted a slice of chocolate cake, rich and dark, with dense frosting. A couple of cups of coffee to go with it. A small bowl of almonds on the side. She had to stop thinking this way, or she'd go even crazier than she already was. No almonds, then. Just the chocolate.

"I called Mike again," Grace admitted, to get her mind off food. "The detective I hired."

"Why?" Robert asked.

"The big seduction scene you suggested," Grace began.

"You want to pay Mike to seduce Rich?"

"Rich likes pussy," Grace said. "Believe me, even if I didn't know from first-hand experience, I have a half-dozen manila envelopes full of proof."

Which you've done nothing with, Gloria said inside Grace's head. What would it take to get rid of her, an exorcism? Peyote? A power drill? The womyn's workshop certainly hadn't done the job. *All talk and no action. I think you're really collecting them because you like them. Honey, it's okay to be a little kinky, but this is revolting. You're getting your kicks looking at pictures of your husband with other women. What other excuse is there? Don't tell Robert you don't like it because he won't believe you. I stopped believing you a long time ago. Nobody stays in this situation if she doesn't like it, or doesn't think she deserves it. I know you don't deserve it, so what does that leave?*

Rich liked pussy, all right. In one revealing series of photos, Mike had captured him inserting Alka-Seltzer tablets into some brunette's vagina before eating her out. In another, he had filled the same woman's twat with white wine from his own mouth. She then straddled him and tinkled Chardonnay all over his face. Mike had even produced photos of the bottle next to the bed: Grgich Hills. Rich's women might be cheap but his wines weren't.

"You're sending the detective to Paris to spy on Rich?"

"If the seduction scene I'm planning for tomorrow night doesn't work, yes," Grace said. "I had him clear his calendar after Tuesday. Rich said he'll be away at least a week. If he doesn't want me back…"

"Then you'll what? Cry some more and not eat for three days? Grace, you're going to have to deal with this sooner or later. It's either that or go nuts. All this stress can't be good for your health."

Grace wanted to slap Robert's face so hard he'd have to peel it off the window and sew it back on his head. Nobody irritated her as much some-one as who was right, and knew it.

"But I'll get thinner."

"You'll end up in the hospital with an IV in your arm."

"Should be good for 15 or 20 pounds. I'll be able wear that red dress I bought in Rome..."

"Jesus Christ, Grace, give the martyr act a rest. Go see this guy Stefan I've been telling you about, if you're serious about losing weight without killing yourself. It's worked for me."

Robert kept staring straight ahead. Grace caught a faint whiff of an ugly idea: what if he'd become too disgusted to look at her? He'd lost – how much? – 30 pounds? 40? A lot. She couldn't see a single stretch mark either. In fact, the more she looked at him, the more she suspected he'd had his neck waxed. Laser treatments, maybe. His five o'clock shadow stopped at his jaw. Nice touch. Rich was always complaining about nicking his neck when he shaved. How had Robert done it? He didn't have that gaunt look sick people get. She thought of lipodystrophy, the bane of men on HIV medication: their faces cave in, and their bellies and upper backs sprout odd humps. Had Robert been HIV-positive all these years, and not told her? Maybe so (shudder to think), and he'd begun taking some nasty new medication, one of those drugs that turn your liver into a gigantic scab af-ter half a dozen pills. But no, that couldn't be it; he didn't have that craggy look. Plus, he'd have told her so. Maybe she'd simply turned him off with her whining and conniving to hold onto a man who was, to be frank with herself, treating her less uxoriously than a used condom. (Condoms at least get fucked before they're discarded.)

135

Or maybe... Stefan the Magic Masseur really existed? Robert *had* lost a lot of weight...

Impossible.

"This is his last chance," Grace said. "I know he'll be home tomorrow night because he'll have to pack. I'm having dinner catered, doing the whole candles and flowers and romantic music routine. All of it. If he doesn't go for it..."

"You'll leave him?"

"If I have to," Grace said. The anvil of her heart pressed down on other organs; for a second, she struggled to breathe. She shut her eyes and leaned against the door. The seat belt cut into her breast but she didn't care. "I really don't want that. I love him so much."

"I know you do, honey," Robert said.

"I want him back. I want it to be like it was when things were good."

"Of course you do."

"And if there's nothing left to salvage – if he really doesn't want me any more – if he's so grossed out by my body – or whatever the hell is going on..." She couldn't make herself finish the thought. She stared out the window and watched arid suburbs unravel. Tract houses gave way to vineyards.

"You'll what?" Robert brought her out of the xeric landscape and back into the passenger seat of her car.

"Divorce his fucking ass," Grace said. She couldn't turn back to look at him. She stared ahead at a faded red minivan with Idaho plates. The minivan's left rear tire looked almost flat, and discolored rectangles suggested the inept removal of bumper stickers. Grace wanted to cry again. She forced herself to take deep breaths until the urge subsided. "If he leaves me no other choice..."

Or you could put those pictures to good use and blackmail him, like you keep threatening to, Gloria offered. *That's a choice you could make. Be sure you explore ALL your options, honey.*

Grace took a nap to escape from her hunger. The scrunching of gravel under the tires woke her up.

She half-expected a bevy of naked nymphets with flowers in their hair to greet them on arrival. None appeared. She didn't know whether to be relieved or disappointed. Clusters of redwoods grew thick on both sides of the main building. Grace heard strains of music and smelled champa incense on the breeze. Birds screeched in the trees. Perfect setting for one of those serial killer movies she'd loved during high school. She blinked and for a dizzy half-second saw glowing filaments woven around the dark green branches. Fluorescent squares and circles floated through the air. The sky looked like a TV image of itself with sunlight reflecting off a dusty picture tube. Grace blinked again and steadied herself. The hallucinations vanished. She needed food, soon, or a couple more of those herbal pep pills.

"The absence of traffic sounds is disconcerting," Robert said.

"I live in Palo Alto. There's no traffic noise there."

"Maybe not in your house, but what about 101 and 280?" Robert asked, opening the trunk to fetch their overnight bags. "It's a constant dull roar in the background, even if you don't notice it when you step outside. You get used to hearing it, and only notice when it's gone."

Grace would need all day Sunday to prepare for her evening with Rich, and had wanted to drive back the same day, but Robert insisted they stay overnight. No point in going to a spa to relax if you exhaust yourself driving up and back, he said, and she couldn't argue with his logic.

At the front desk, instead of a hearty blonde mountain wench with a name like Olga or Lavender, a petite Asian woman whose discreet gold name tag read HYUN checked them in. Hyun's head only rose about two inches above the reception desk. Grace found this endearing, and was further charmed by Hyun's Australian accent.

You want so desperately to dislike this experience, Gloria said. *Just like you wanted to hate the women at the gym. Why do you keep expecting people to be disagreeable? Is it just because of how you look? Have you thought about that? Maybe that's why you let Rich go around with all those other women, when you could have done something about it months ago? Because you think you deserve it? You have no idea how pathetic you are, Grace. Sometimes I'm ashamed to call you my daughter...*

"Shut up!" Grace said.

Hyun and Robert stopped talking, and looked at her.

What had they been saying? Grace groped for clarity. Their rooms. She'd heard a snatch of conversation about their rooms. They'd each get their own little cabin.

"Our own cabins? No way!" Grace tried to sound cheerful and amazed. Moving to Northern California from North Carolina, the local use of *shut up* to mean *I don't believe it* or *Are you kidding* caught her off guard more often than not. It was meant to be affirming but Grace heard the words as rude for at least a year. "I thought you'd be booked solid this time of year!"

Hyun's extra second before replying told Grace she'd been let off the hook, but not believed: "Your brother made reservations last week, and we had a cancellation. It was perfect timing."

Robert accepted keys for them both.

"I'll have Dolores escort you to your cabins," Hyun said. She handed Robert two folded sheets of paper fresh from her iMac's printer. "And here are your schedules. If you want to change them or sign up for something else, just call me here at the front desk. The refectory is open until midnight, and room service is available until that time. Enjoy your stay."

Hyun smiled at Robert. Her smile at Grace burned a few watts cooler.

A svelte Hispanic woman waved from a doorway and gestured for them to follow her. Grace wondered how she could leave this place feeling refreshed and rejuvenated when all the employees she'd seen were no larger than a size 8.

*

On the way to her cabin (cabin-ette? cabinet?), Grace passed a group of four women walking in the opposite direction, toward the main building. All wore loose, flowing dresses and, from the way things up front were jiggling, not a single bra among them. The breeze was brisk and cool enough to... well, their high-beams were on. Rich would love this: bosomy sluts in the woods. Thin ones, at that.

Grace turned to watch them pass. They giggled at something (*me, I assume*) and one of them, a brunette, stroked her companion's back: this woman's narrow waistline gave way to a heart-shaped swell of hips. The four women giggled again, almost out of earshot now. This time the brunette turned back and sent a nauseating look of pity Grace's way. Grace stopped cold and would have screamed if there had been any emotion left in her. The only hourglass figure she felt like seeing at the moment was the red one on a black widow spider's back just before she dropped it down this bitch's dress.

Grace hurried down the path to her cabinet.

*

It's the only thing you think about any more, Gloria said.

"Shut up!" Grace curled into a fetal ball on her unfamiliar bed and pulled the pillow over her head. The linens smelled fresh, as if they'd been laundered with organic detergent and line-dried in a sunny meadow miles from the nearest freeway. Grace smelled lavender and a hint of rose, very comforting.

You only think about one thing: losing weight so you can get Rich back. If you lose 20 pounds in a hurry, he'll notice you again. So you take diuretics to piss out every last drop of water and you take herbal speed to keep from eating. Now you're here for a weekend of relaxation but what good is it going to do you? You're so strung out, you're about to explode.

"Shut up!"

No, I will not shut up. You listen to me. Throw away the goddamn pills. Go get a massage. Get a body wrap. Soak in one of those vats of mineralized mud. It may look like a tub of boiling shit but it's better than what you're doing to yourself. Eat some healthy food. Take a yoga class and stretch yourself out. I don't care what you do, but you're starting to scare me. You're putting him first. You need to put you first. You. Do you hear what I'm saying? You're too damn smart to have such a lack of willpower…

"Shut up!"

Gloria subsided.

Grace didn't budge until she heard a knock at the door.

"I booked us a stretching and breathing workshop," Robert said from outside. "We should get going if we're going to make it!"

With effort, Grace sat up in bed. In an abstract way she liked the décor of her cabinet: hardwood floors, simple rustic furniture, a squashy armchair with a reading lamp next to it, fresh wildflowers in a blown-glass vase. A framed picture of a small boy on a beach took her mind off herself for a few additional seconds. She didn't know she'd been crying until she scratched an itchy a spot on her cheek and felt moisture. She looked around the room again, saw her overnight bag and her purse on the low dresser by the window, and shut her eyes. Her head spun. She clutched the bedclothes with unsteady hands.

She could do this.

She could get through this.

Maybe.

*

Nobody with a strangely hyphenated name encouraged the stretching – breathing workshop participants to cry as they felt the need. Nobody led a conga line around the room with her anal cavity, or any other body part for that matter. This encouraged Grace. She took a position on the mat next to Robert – ungracefully dropping the last six inches to the floor, which smacked her bottom and left her a bit winded – and tried to relax. Instead of repeating the mantras the workshop instructor chanted, Grace toyed with various tautologies:

The instructor is calm because she is thin.

The instructor is thin because she is calm.

If I were calmer, then I would be thinner.

If I were thinner, then I would be calmer.

After several minutes of this, Grace felt almost peaceful.

*

Robert dragged her to an introductory yoga class next, which involved trying to wrench her appendages into contortions extreme by even Torquemada's standards. She kept hoping her appetite would go away. She kept hoping her hands would stop shaking. Her leg muscles worked about as well as Play Doh when she tried to stand up after the yoga session, and she leaned on Robert for support. His bulging eyes told her how much she still weighed.

Grace had an appointment for a purifying body wrap next. Walking past the refectory, heavenly smells beckoned – she imagined sausages, steamed vegetables, fresh fruit, a pitcher of fresh-squeezed orange juice, and a pot of coffee. Organic seven-grain toast smeared with butter and honey, with a little cinnamon sprinkled over it. Her mouth watered. She wiped moisture off her lower lip with the back of her hand. The motion brought an eddy of unshowered underarm smells to her nose, though, and she stopped in her tracks. Should she dash back to the cabinet for a fast shower? Should she stop in the cafeteria for a bite to eat? Grace discreetly sniffed her pits and decided she smelled about as appetizing as roadkill sashimi. No way could she subject an herbal wrapper to her unwashed corpus. Granted, this was Northern California and the spa staff probably got off on the smell of sweat (*Like, it's natural, you know? It's just, you know, like, this natural thing, and it's something we all have in common. It's our common humanity. Bodies have smells, and it's just, like, a fact of life, man. Smells unite us. Want an enema?*), but for a displaced debutante from North Carolina, stench was not an option.

No food, then. At least I'll be lying very still for the herbal wrap.

The herbal wrap would be great if you were a dead Egyptian, Grace concluded halfway through. She couldn't move without dislodging a swatch of gauze that had been soaked in green tea and tea tree oil and goat urine and pitchblende and various other arcane substances. The cucumber slices over her eyes smelled like a salad left too long in the sun. She'd never liked cucumber to eat, much less to wear, but she kept her mouth shut and tried to keep her thoughts flowing in a straight line. They kept tangling up, breaking into fragments, and dissolving before she could grasp them.

After the wrap, she begged off the aerobics class Robert had booked. She needed to be alone. Everyone in sight oppressed her with slenderness.

If one more skinny bitch so much as blinked at her, Grace was going to kill. She felt too raw for all this relaxation. Spas like this only worked for people who had already crossed the finish line, the ones who could parade naked in public without fear of inciting mass nausea or mob violence. The ones whose bodies wouldn't make small children laugh, or cry. Grace wanted to hide. To soak in the tub. To get the smell of this holistic herbal crap out of her pores. If she had to coat her skin with anything, it might as well be MAC or Aveda. Even motor oil, as far as she knew, would smell better.

Robert wouldn't hear of her missing the mud soak, though. The minerals, he said. Their skin needed the minerals. The mud was purifying. It would help them get rid of accumulated toxins. *Like Rich's other women? Now there's an accumulation of toxins for you.* Robert woke her up an hour later, dragged her to the refectory for a bite of food, and, after cautioning her to eat something light so she wouldn't fart in the mud tub (who would notice?), devoured enough stir-fried vegetables and brown rice to kill a horse. Grace nibbled. Her head seemed to clear a bit.

"Ooh! Hot!" She squawked when she probed the bubbling poo (that's how it looked, and didn't smell much better) with a toe.

Robert had shamelessly stripped off his towel and stepped into his vat.

Less shocking than the sight of his penis was the sight of his abdomen, or lack thereof. She'd seen Robert nude before. So had hundreds of other people, from the way he talked. And he might possibly be better-hung than her husband, from the look of things, but she didn't want to go there. He'd lost weight without sagging. He had no loose skin, no stretch marks. He looked as if he'd never had a paunch in the first place, or as if he might be slowly growing one, not losing it. She couldn't see his abs but when she looked at him, *chubby* didn't instantly spring to mind, either.

Robert settled into the mud. His facial features melted into a look of sublime contentment.

"You've got to try this," he said.

Reluctantly, Grace placed her towel on the deck beside her mudbath. She covered her breasts with one hand and her privates with the other, then lowered herself into the mud. *Glorp*, went the mud. *Glorp glorp. Glorp.*

She had enough time to think *this is really quite hot*, and then she felt very tired.

Next thing she knew, someone was hauling her out of the mud. A circle of people gathered around, looking worried.

Robert was still naked, and covered with mud.

Looks like he's been dipped in shit, Grace thought, and closed her eyes.

She woke up in the hospital.

CHAPTER TWELVE:

ROBERT

Hospital interlude, with leeks. The Northern California weather.
An invitation.

Grace lay half-conscious in her hospital bed, the light green gown bunching at her armpits, an IV dripping nutrients and fluids into her arm. He pulled the thin blue blanket over her and wondered how many patients had vomited on it. Weren't contaminated linens supposed to be incinerated? Was her bed a biohazard? He couldn't see any telltale stains on the fabric but that didn't mean they weren't there.

"What time is it?" Grace asked.

Her weak voice broke Robert's heart. She sounded like an organ donor. After donating.

"Ten."

"Oh shit," she said. "I feel so bad."

Robert said nothing. What was there to say? *You deserve it for not eating? It's a miracle you didn't drown in that vat of mud? We almost couldn't pull you out?*

"I called Rich and got his voice mail," he said. "I also called Flora Trust and Gloria. Used your phone while you were unconscious. Neither of them answered, by the way. I assume they'll call back when they check their messages."

"Voice mail," Grace said. She shut her eyes and shook her head, either in wonder or disgust or some weary combination of the two. "Can I have some ginger ale?"

Robert looked around the room, then caught himself in a stupid moment. Hospital rooms don't have minibars.

"I'll buzz the nurse," he said.

When Grace fell asleep again, Robert went for a walk. He took her cell phone as well as his own, thinking he'd make a few calls from the parking lot. He didn't entirely believe cellular signals disrupted medical equipment but didn't want any deaths on his conscience, either. He also wanted a break from the beeps and roars and groans of the hospital, and he craved a breath of air that didn't smell like disinfectant.

Guilt gnawed at Robert's stomach like rats in ripe trash. He should have insisted she see Stefan. Should have thrown a conniption fit, in fact, at her first sign of refusal. Grace had lost weight, all right. *Be careful what you wish for; you might get it.* She'd been lowballing. Fifteen pounds in a week's time, not seven, as she'd claimed. This came out when Grace woke up enough to answer a few questions. Not healthy at all. Robert felt guilty because he looked so good in comparison. He'd lost 40 pounds and while he didn't think he'd be modeling underwear any time soon, and still saw himself as fat, he couldn't win an argument with his mirror. Every time he passed a storefront and looked at himself, he asked himself *How is this me?* Every time he stood up and sat down, he didn't struggle with the dead weight of a gut hanging off the front of his body. He no longer approached staircases with a mix of dread and resignation. His knees liked him better these days, and his feet didn't hurt. Gravity still sucked, but it didn't swallow. But Grace… she was already in a fragile state of mind. Without meaning to, he'd pushed her over the edge. She'd cracked. Perhaps she'd shattered. Who would tape the pieces back together?

Stefan, he thought. *I know he'll see her.*

The question of cost reared its ugly head again. Robert had asked Stefan twice how much this transformation would cost. Stefan's cryptic answer – *You can afford it* – didn't reassure him; it unsettled him.

Grace can afford it, Robert thought.

Their father had done well for himself before his death two decades ago. He left Gloria more money than even she could spend, and he'd set up modest trust funds for the kids. Robert's own inheritance had knocked out his student loans. What was left wouldn't allow him to quit his job and retire to a villa on the Amalfi Coast. Yet. Well, he could, but he had chosen to invest. He already earned plenty as an attorney. And if he lost this job, he could afford to coast for a while. He doubted Stefan wanted money, however. Anyone with the power to reshape living flesh would never go begging. Whatever Stefan wanted, it had to be something he didn't already have, something he couldn't obtain for himself.

Grace can afford it, whatever it is. And it's not like I'm broke and starving.

When Robert called Flora Trust and Gloria again, neither one answered the phone. Robert supposed Gloria and her lover had taken off again for parts unknown: Cuba, Antarctica, Tibet, you never knew where those two would end up. On some level this made him feel squirmy – Juan wasn't *that* much older than Robert – but he didn't let himself think about it for long. As far as Flora Trust was concerned, Robert didn't care to contemplate what or whom she might be doing. He couldn't decide what was worse, the physical logistics of it or their (loud) postcoital conversation, which would inevitably be about collectivist politics or vegan diets or whale migration or the status of oppressed peoples. Did this make him a misogynist? Or just one of the last soldiers standing in the battle for aesthetically pleasing sex? He thought, *It's all right to be ugly while you fuck, but before you get started, you need to look good.*

*

He called James, and by some miracle got him on the second ring:

"You're home?"

"Where else would I be?" James sounded morose. Robert could picture the sack-cloth and ashes. "I went to see Stefan about it but there isn't a lot he can do. He said *I could stick my fingers in your brain and twirl it around like a bowl of custard, but you wouldn't like me very much after that.*"

"What does that mean?"

"I don't know. He said something about ruptured psychological frameworks. That made even less sense than the custard. I'm not going back to see him, Robert. He's done all he can."

"Wha…" Competing questions fought to be the first out of Robert's mouth. "You what?"

"I'm not going back to see him. I'm miserable, and the better I look, the worse I feel. It's not a panacea, Robert."

Robert watched a fortyish man push an elderly woman in a wheelchair toward the hospital entrance. The man's wide, creased face and thick mustache reminded Robert of truckers at rest stops – the kind of people he'd take a leak next to on road trips and wonder how they could be from the same country. The woman listed to one side. Her coughing was audible, even from a distance. What was wrong with her? Was it contagious? Electric doors slid open to admit them. The intersection of their lives ended when the doors slid shut again.

"You're perfect, James. There's no reason to be miserable. Don't you see that? You never needed Stefan in the first place. If you want to stop seeing him, then stop. You won't gain weight again. Your dick won't shrink down to nothingness. Speaking of nothingness, Christ, that reminds me, I haven't eaten all day."

"Nice to have Stefan around, isn't it?" James's sarcasm caught Robert off guard. "You could eat pizza and ice cream all day and still look like an Abercrombie & Fitch model. I now have 4% body fat. I had one of those calipers tests done at the gym."

"Grace is sick," Robert cut James off. "I'm calling from the hospital. Grace went on some stupid starvation diet, strung herself out on pills, went nuts, and passed out in a mud bath. She'd have drowned in it if I hadn't been there."

"Holy shit!"

"Literally. We were both covered in mineralized mud."

"So what happened next?"

"Somebody called 911 and took her to the hospital. She's in a room now. They're keeping her overnight for observation. They'll let her go tomorrow if her electrolytes come back to a decent level."

James said that was scary and Robert agreed. "She's always been a little weird where food was concerned. When she was about thirteen, she decided – and don't ask me where this idea came from – it was only healthy to eat white food. Kind of freaked us all out, except for our father, who never noticed anything unless you hit him in the head with it. Grace ate nothing but popcorn, white bread, leeks, and spoons of sugar. There was something else... oh yeah, cauliflower. Lots of cauliflower. She drank milk. It lasted about a week. She puked in class one day and had stay home for a few days until her system sorted itself out. She flirted with bulimia but didn't like the puking. She said vomit's overrated."

"It's not my favorite thing to do either," James said.

"Yeah. If it's not one thing with her, it's another. I always thought sex was the best anesthetic, and after sex, it's money. With her, it's food."

"So when are you coming home?"

"Tomorrow morning, I hope."

"Call me when you get here," James said.

"I will." Robert swallowed the lump in his throat and said the words he wanted to stifle. "I miss you."

An excruciating pause later, James said, "That's sweet. I miss you too."

But not in the same way, Robert thought. *How had Grace dealt with that reaction from Rich all this time, without falling apart years ago?* His mind held its breath in the aftermath of that idea. He held the phone away from his head and stared at it, as if it had bitten him or burned his hand. He disconnected the call without another word.

*

Robert paced the parking lot in a funk. He told himself, *I don't want these feelings for James.* But he didn't believe himself and couldn't let go. Could Stefan scoop them out like a palm full of fat cells? Was obsession, like obesity, curable? Robert had his doubts. The balminess of the evening compounded his miseries. When the night air feels like a kiss, the mix of loneliness and one-sided affection is worse than anything the madmen of the Inquisition might have dreamt up. Robert stood next to a pot of jasmine and took deep breaths. If he breathed deeply enough, he'd line his sinuses with jasmine molecules: defense against the odors of the sick. Something to think about for a few seconds, other than James.

Robert shrugged at the futility of all this. So much for not thinking about him. It was like resolving not to breathe.

Better go back in. Grace might wake up and freak out because I'm not there. I need to eat, and the hospital's actually less dismal than the parking lot.

Why had nobody warned him about the insidious torture of Northern California's perfect weather? All that sun has its dark side.

It's a great place to be single because in a climate like this, everybody wants to get laid. It's a terrible place to be ugly because you miss out on all the sex. And it's the worst place in the world to be in love with somebody who doesn't love you back...

Robert stopped dead. A nurse passing by, pushing an empty wheelchair, stopped did a double-take. She asked if he was okay.

"I'm fine, thanks," he said in a strangled voice.

"You sure? You look pale. Need a ride in this thing?"

Robert shook his head.

"I'm fine, really. Long day, not enough sleep. You know how that can be."

The nurse, who looked like a soccer mom in ER scrubs, nodded. Robert imagined her riding herd on three or four children. She drove a Ford minivan. She and her husband were going nuts chasing after their kids and their schedules. Soccer, piano lessons, academic bowl, ballet, and so forth. He couldn't understand how people did it, and why. Didn't would-be parents know what they were getting themselves into? Did they not realize they wouldn't have a second of free time for the next quarter-century? Or was that the appeal – they couldn't come up with anything more original to do?

"You take care, okay? If you're here with somebody else, you won't be any good to them if you fall apart," Soccer Mom said. She wagged a finger at him and smiled. "Now you promise me you'll get some rest and I'll leave you alone. Promise?"

Robert nodded. This time, he didn't cross his fingers behind his back. The nurse said good night and departed with another smile.

I'm in love with James. Oh fuck. That's the worst thing in the world. It's not just a crush on him.

He could almost hear Grace saying *It took you long enough to figure that out!* Flora Trust would bellow DUH at the top of her lungs, burst out laughing, fall to the floor, and pee on herself.

I hate my job and I love James. Why am I always the last to figure these things out?

Robert had not boiled it down to this before, not in its simplest terms. He'd been hurt enough the first time. He stood in the hallway and looked at gruesome medical history posters: doctors administering squalling children shots with needles the size of turkey basters, festering boils on feverish skin, burn victims in tattered dressings. Blinded eyes, broken bones. Petri dish cultures teeming with bacterial malevolence. How was anyone sick supposed to recover if subjected to a horror show like this every time they walked the halls? James would love this display but nobody else in their right mind would be able to stomach it for long.

I'm in love with James. Who doesn't love me back.

It wasn't a crush and it wasn't an infatuation. Robert had no idea where the boundaries between those concepts lay, much less between the neighboring republics of *love* and *in love with*. Maybe they fit together like the countries on the Arabian Peninsula. Nobody cared where Saudi Arabia ended and Yemen began because in the dead sand of the Empty Quarter, what difference did it make? Crush, love, infatuation – Robert had visited them all repeatedly but never studied a map. He had the passport stamps but no green card. And now (why was he always the last to know these things?) he was in love with James.

Who didn't love him back.

This is horrible, Robert thought. *I've got to talk to him about it when I get home. I'll go fucking nuts if I don't. Assuming I'm not already there.*

What qualified as nuts, anyway? Robert considered definitions and couldn't come up with anything specific. Pecans, cashews, pistachios, dementia, psychosis. Why didn't he know any psychologists? Everybody should be able to count a shrink or two among their friends. He knew too many lawyers, and lawyers could be counted on not to know anything about anything. It was their job to dismantle knowledge.

In the cafeteria, Robert distracted himself with an array of unappetizing food choices. Did he want the shrink-wrapped ham sandwich or the shrink-wrapped bean burrito? Hmm. The shrink-wrapped cheese croissant looked alluring. Relatively. He reframed the question: Did he want the salmonella or the botulism? A bowl of apples didn't appeal to him, either. They'd have a texture like compressed talcum powder and wouldn't taste much better. After a few minutes of this, he gave up. He could afford to indulge in processed crap. At the spa, he'd eaten nothing but wholesome food: tofu, brown rice, vegetables. Why not go for the Doritos, a Milky Way bar, and a bottle of decaffeinated Coke? He'd earned the privilege. Sin and redemption, backward.

A male nurse (did doctors wear green scrubs and work this late at night?) at the opposite table caught Robert's eye. Nothing else in the tastefully bland cafeteria did. Thick dark hair, razor stubble, soul patch, glasses with sideways-oval frames. Quite nice. Eyebrows too carefully shaped, though. (What the hell, everyone was allowed to have a flaw.) Both ears sported a couple of small hoops each. Robert sipped his Coke and watched the nurse read a magazine and munch a Clif Bar.

Out of my league, Robert thought.

The guy looked up, made eye contact. Kept staring.

Maybe not, Robert thought.

In any case, he didn't expect to find himself following the nurse into a storage closet five minutes later. They never spoke a word. Glances were enough. The guy nodded *follow me* and Robert did. Nobody saw them.

"Should we be doing this?" Robert asked.

"Why not? You're cute, we're both here, I'm on break, I can tell you want to. It's late at night. Nobody else is around... do I have to keep giving reasons or are you going to fuck me?"

Robert nodded. He didn't know what to say.

"Use this," the nurse, whose name tag said Cesar, said, handing Robert a tube from a supply shelf.

He stole a glance: surgical-grade lubricating gel. He had fallen off the edge of the world into the precipice he'd always wanted to inhabit. Now that he was here, he didn't know what to do. It was like studying Spanish for years and not knowing how to answer ¿como estas? Your first day in Mexico.

Great, Robert thought, squeezing some lube onto his fingertips.

"Here." The nurse handed Robert a condom in a packet. "I'm clean, but, you know..."

He wondered, *Aren't we supposed to kiss first?* His fingers encountered minimal resistance, and after some probing, Robert put on the proffered condom, lubricated and positioned himself, gripped Cesar's hips, and slid inside.

You're so hot...

(I am?)

Man, you must not know how fucking hot you are... so good... fuck me... slower, slower, easy... like that... so good yeah...

The tattoo at the base of Cesar's spine caught Robert's eye. An ornate cross, from the look of it, although Robert couldn't bend his head far enough forward to get a better view without giving himself whiplash.

Stop a minute... don't move... you feel so good inside me... just wanna feel you for a minute...

Robert thought of James saying the same thing once in bed, and the moment broke in two. He thought, *I want to be with James. I don't want to be doing this. Oh my God, what am I doing?*

He'd never been picked up like this before, not once in all his years in San Francisco, where sex dripped like rain from the branches of the trees. Everyone seemed to have a woody or a wet cunt at all times. He'd always been left out of the simmering orgy that is the Bay Area, and now Cesar wanted to invite him in...

And Cesar was moaning *fuck me, fuck me* as Robert thrust inside him, harder and harder, pushing all thoughts of James out of his head, or trying to with little success. Robert pounded into Cesar and the medical supply cart they were leaning against for support banged rhythmically against the wall and Robert thought they'd wake the corpses in the morgue if they made any more noise than this...

Robert thought, *I want to be with James...*

A second later, he felt hot semen in the palm he'd wrapped around Cesar's cock. On impulse, brought the hand to his mouth for a taste. Salty. Nice. And it didn't have the desired effect of pushing James out of his head.

I can't deal with this, Robert thought, withdrawing from Cesar's body. *He doesn't even care that I didn't finish.*

"That was hot," Cesar said. "I needed that."

Robert nodded.

You could ask whether I came or not.

"Here are some wipes," Cesar said.

Robert cleaned himself off and hurried back to Grace's room. He dropped the slip of paper upon which Cesar had written a phone number and an e-mail address into the first garbage can he saw. He wanted a shower. He wanted James. He wanted to cry.

CHAPTER THIRTEEN:
GRACE

Grace's favorite kind of nut. Orchids. The seduction.

"You can't leave now," said the doctor on duty. "It's too soon. Those diet pills made a mess of your electrolyte levels." He went on to tell Grace she needed another full day of rest, another round of blood tests. Grace let the words zoom over her head like the jets she could see in the distance when she looked out her window.

Gloria might have cautioned, *Never stand between a Southern woman and her man. Not if you don't want your guts punctured by her high heels when she knocks you on your ass and walks right over you.*

Grace had left her heels at home – hadn't worn them in years; they hurt her feet too much at her present weight – but could achieve the same effect effortlessly (with everyone but her husband). Even in this diminished state, wearing no makeup, she only had to lift one eyebrow and flatten her mouth in a hard straight line.

"You want me to *what*? I'm not sure I heard you correctly."

"Stay another 24 hours for observation. Perhaps in psych," said the doctor, the desiccated sort of MD who spends his rare free days on the golf course and fills up with high-octane bourbon at the country club afterward.

"Not an option," Grace said. God, what she'd forfeit in catering charges. "I appreciate your concern, I really do, but I'm just fine. Just needed a little food and rest. I must have picked up a bug."

The doctor shook his head. He might have been handsome once, before running the gauntlet of medical school, medical practice, medical marriage, and at least one medical divorce. He had the kicked-dog look of a man who has lost a couple of wives, expensively.

Robert, Grace noticed out of the corner of one eye, had stepped back and was trying to press himself into the wall.

"You don't have a bug," the doctor said. "You were dangerously dehydrated and on the verge of malnutrition. I understand trying to lose weight, but has nobody told you not to try it all at once?"

"I've heard everything by now," Grace said. "Two or three times. At least. And I really do need to get home. I have something pressing going on tonight. If I'm not at death's door, I can't miss it."

"More pressing than your health? You're not at death's door now, but you could be."

Grace's eyebrow rose once again.

"I'll let you go on one condition," the doctor said. How many of his ex-wives had used the very same words before walking out? Grace imagined him with a 23-year-old on his arm: he looked the right age to be dating women younger than his daughters. "You see your primary care physician as early next week as you can get an appointment. And in the meantime, you have to rest. No more diet pills. No starvation diets. No stress."

"That sounds like more than one condition," Grace said. Any minute now, he was going to hand her a contract to sign in blood. He'd have a phlebotomist tap a vein for fresh ink.

"Call it however you see it. I want you to take care of yourself. This can't be allowed to happen again. Your health is at risk, Grace. I hope you understand that."

Grace understood it perfectly well. But when your entire way of life is on the chopping block, when you're going to lose your husband and all the years you've shared together, doesn't your desperation justify a few risks? She nodded and smiled at the doctor, promised him she'd take extra good care of herself in the next few days, deflated the second he left the room, and had to shut her eyes until a few sparks of energy returned. It was barely 11.00, and she craved a nap. More than that, she wanted the goddamn IV taken out of her arm. If a nurse didn't withdraw it soon, she'd do it herself.

"Get me the fuck out of here," she said to Robert.

*

Robert stopped at the first convenience store they passed.

"Stay here," he said.

A few minutes later he emerged with a quart-sized bottle of green Gatorade and a package of cashews, which were her favorite type of nut after Mary Rose.

"Drink this on the way home," he said, handing it to her.

Grace started to squawk in protest but recognized the courtroom look in his eye.

"I'll have to pee every 20 minutes," she cautioned.

"I doubt that, but it doesn't matter," Robert said. "We'll stop every 20 minutes if we have to. You're not going to collapse on the way home, you hear me?"

"People can't collapse if they're sitting down," Grace said. "I might slump over, but if it happens, I promise to do it quietly." She drifted for a few seconds. Had anything ever tasted as good as this Gatorade? "You know, if I ever get married again, it should be to a gay guy. I'm already not getting sex from my heterosexual husband, so that part wouldn't be any different. At least..." For fuck's sake, she was welling up. Her throat tied itself in a knot. She took a swig of Gatorade, dribbled a little down her chin, and let herself relax for a second. "At least I'd be treated well, don't you think?"

"You couldn't do much worse," Robert said.

*

Rich wouldn't be home before six but with an early flight to Paris in the morning, he wouldn't be home much later, either. Although she hated few things more than the sound of the front door swinging shut in an empty house, today she enjoyed the silence. She felt too light-headed and rubbery to accomplish much, but that's what checkbooks and cater-waiters were for. She'd hired a decorator to handle the candles and flowers. In theory, everything ought to be perfect. However, in theory, bumblebees and helicopters ought not to fly.

"You're sure you're okay to drive back to Palo Alto?" Robert had asked, when they pulled up in front of his building.

"Do I have a choice?"

"I know, decorators at three, caterers at four, but Grace, listen. At the risk of being too personal..."

"That's possible?"

Robert shrugged. "I just wondered if... tonight... the whole seduction thing. Are you sure you're up for it?"

"Do I get any choice in the matter?"

"You can't take chances with your health, Grace."

"How healthy is divorce?"

Robert sank into one of his troubled silences. Grace took advantage of the moment to slip behind the wheel of her car, blow him a kiss, and leave stripes of smoking rubber on the pavement in front of his building. She stole a look in the rear-view mirror and got a nanosecond's glimpse of him standing on the sidewalk with his mouth hanging open.

We always did think he was a little touched, didn't we, honey? Gloria said. *At least you didn't tell him everything you've got up your sleeve… not that you ever have.*

*

Things the decorator said:

The sconces are all wrong. You should never have installed them in a house with this overall décor. They don't cast light anywhere useful, and it's almost impossible to harmonize them in terms of the whole feng shui flow effect. The energies. You know, they don't harmonize. They just don't. I'm sorry. I think you should take out the sconces at once. Grace thought: *Before Rich gets home?*

Only certain flowers will do. Flower arrangement is an art. I didn't bring flowers with me because we have to discuss the sort of energies you want them to impart to the space. The scenario, you know. The whole scenario. I understand this is a seductive dinner? Lilies just do not seduce me. Bulb flowers do not seduce me. They just don't. I'm sorry, but they don't. I think you need orchids. Yes. Definitely orchids. They look like vaginas, don't you think? Or little penises? You definitely need orchids. How much of a budget do we have, and which rooms do we want to target? Oh wait, we discussed that already, I have it here in my notebook, never mind. The kitchen? Dining area? The bedroom? I think we need to have little fragrant penises and vaginas scattered suggestively around the living space. For the erotic ambience. It's perfect, isn't it? I know just the place to get them. Grace thought: *I think only one penis and one vagina will be necessary*

160

tonight. Can I get you out of here before you whip out a tube of K-Y Jelly and squirt it all over the chairs to heighten that slippery erotic feeling? Maybe some glitter and rose petals sprinkled in the erotic goo, for effect? You fucking freak.

Candles are so overdone. They just melt and get wax all over everything. Candle poo everywhere. Every time I see a movie and there's this big seduction scene, you know, and there are candles everywhere, I'm like, *Ew, all that candle poo. And don't these people ever set things on fire by accident?* I mean, there you are, boning away, and the covers come off the bed. Don't they go up in flames? Wait, they did that in the movie *Go,* did you see that? So they got it right in one movie, but that's the exception that proves the rule. Candles are overdone. What you need is a few strategic oil lamps. They smell better than candles when you blow them out. Trust me on this one. They smell better, and there's no wax. The quality of the light is almost indistinguishable. Trust me. Grace thought: *Oil lamps. And will you scream much when I pour the remaining oil over your body and toss a lit match in your direction?*

I can't believe you ordered Middle Eastern food from the caterers. Doesn't hummus make you gassy? It does me. Baba ghanouj, too. How on earth can you stage a big seduction scene when you're… oh my God, excuse me, you must think I'm so vulgar. I just can't help it. It's true. I just love hummus, it's like my favorite food on earth, and like, I always eat too much of it. Give me some celery sticks and a bowl of hummus and I'll eat it right up! Every last bit! And let me tell you, seduction is out of the question for the next two days! You just can't be seductive while you're squeezing your cheeks together to pinch back a…

Grace said: "Get the *fuck* out of my house."

*

Just go to Pier One and Whole Foods, honey, Gloria said. *You have more taste than that pale skinny bitch in her grey granny sweater and cat's-eye glasses could ever dream of. And who did her makeup? Did you see that? She put it on with a spatula! Her blusher looked like a third-degree burn from the neck up. She calls herself a decorator? You're better off without trash like that. You're a Southern woman and that's all it takes. I would know because I taught you myself. Give your decorator a little credit and buy an oil lamp, but otherwise it's up to you. It's your house. It's your life. Rich is your husband. You figure it out.*

Grace wanted to lie down and pretend the rest of the world didn't exist. At moments like this, she wanted her extra-dimensional panic room. She wanted to fast forward through the part where she spread Mike's incriminating photos across the dining room table and, when Rich got home, told him exactly what she wanted, when she wanted it, and in what position. She wanted to cut straight to the part where Rich lay on top of her and looked deep into her eyes as he entered her body. Slowly, slowly, until he was inside her up to the hilt. She wanted to hide in her secret room until the time he'd whisper the words *a little bit stinky and a little bit kinky* in her ear, or, even better, *I love you so much.* At which point she'd be quite happy if he rolled her over and pounded her from behind, doggie style. Anything. As long as he was doing it, and meant it, and she could go to sleep afterward.

Maybe those hospital people knew what they were talking about.

Grace brewed a cup of Darjeeling tea, drank it too hot, and rushed out to buy flowers and an oil lamp before the stores closed.

*

Rich should have been home by six. In their college days he might have thrown clothes in the approximate direction of a suitcase but now his suits needed not to be crumpled. He'd be away at least a week, possibly two. He'd need time to pick out ties, cuff links, underwear. How many pairs of shoes? Which shirts? He didn't sink to the same depths of detail as Robert (did anyone?) but for a straight man he could be surgically fussy.

So where the fuck was he?

Grace looked at the microwave clock. Then she looked at her cell phone. She looked back at the microwave clock. Her eyes stung. She blinked. 7.43 arrived. Rich didn't.

Bowls of hummus and baba ghanouj perfumed the air with garlic. The pita wedges wilted. She wondered how to revive them. Whether it was worth it. On what level did these flat triangles of dough symbolize her marriage? She picked one up, shook it between her fingers to see how flimsy it had become after three hours on her countertop, and ate it dry. A smudge of either dip would have been nice but the dry bread made her think of communion. *This is my body...* Fortunately Gloria had never gotten into the religion thing. Grace poured herself a glass of Pinot. *This is my blood.* Hadn't Robert's friend James been a bit of a religious freak at one point? She thought back. Vague memories surfaced. Robert said James had always been an altar boy at heart. Poor thing. Lecherous priests, Catholic guilt, lifelong scars. Psychologically he was still walking funny, Robert had gone on to say. Rich had never been religious and between the sheets, it showed. He'd do anything... except, lately, fuck his wife. With a sip of wine, Grace washed down a bite of pita. It was like swallowing a sliver of dried sponge. Now she knew how futility tasted.

She spritzed the bouquets of flowers in the kitchen, the dining room, the living room, and the bedroom. Gerbera daisies were completely underrated as tools of seduction, she decided. The bold pink and orange blossoms demanded attention. Anything colorful was inherently sensual, just because. Orchids? She didn't think the stems she chose (big white blos-

163

soms) looked the least bit phallic or vaginal, but they reminded her of naughty Mapplethorpe photos from one of Robert's coffee table books. She put them in the bedroom. Rich wouldn't catch the reference but he didn't need to. Maybe she'd absorb some erotic energy from them and give Rich the fuck of the century. Make him forget those other women.

After all, she'd lost 15 pounds. She was looking relatively thin, and makeup would conceal the dark circles under her eyes, mostly.

She drank more wine and waited. He couldn't stay out all night, not before a trip to Europe. He hadn't already been home and packed; she checked to make sure as soon as she walked in the door. No point staging a big seduction if he was on a plane somewhere over the Atlantic Ocean. Or was this just an ultimatum? And which label scared her more?

He'll be here soon enough, Grace reassured herself. She refilled her glass. Shit, she needed to open a new bottle. *At least it'll give me something to do, other than calling Robert to bitch.*

Gloria said, *Just don't call Rich. Do not, under any circumstances, call Rich. You can't seduce a man after you've yelled at him for not coming home when he was supposed to.*

For once, Grace had to concede that her mother's disembodied voice might have a point.

*

She had arranged the photographs decoratively around the dishes on the dining room table. From the kitchen, the table would be visible but not obvious. He'd notice it but she'd have time to steer him in that direction when she felt they were ready to go there. But the pictures themselves... if she had a way of quilting them together at the edges, she could have made a tablecloth out of them. There were so many. Here was Rich doing it with that woman from the trattoria, missionary position. What was her name again? Monica? Grace squinted at the photo. Wasn't that one of the cheap hotels in South of Market? She couldn't keep his bimbos straight. And here he was with the bottle of wine. How did that slut hold still while he spat Chardonnay up her snatch? Was this how cars felt, getting an oil change? No matter how thrilling it might have been to imagine, Grace would have shrieked with laughter and fallen off the bed.

Which is probably why it was happening to some other woman and not you, Gloria pointed out.

Go fuck yourself, Grace said. She took another drink of wine and laid out photos like playing cards. Concentration. Uno. Go fish.

Rich, with a black woman. When was this? Grace stared at the picture, racked her brain for details, couldn't recall the circumstances. Maybe this woman had been one of the first dalliances Mike photographed. Hard to say. Grace had a notebook somewhere but couldn't be bothered to find it. She fanned half a dozen photos of the same woman across the tabletop, then moved on to the next tramp in the stack.

Forty-five minutes later, when Rich arrived, Grace was still fiddling with the pictures. She had finished half the new bottle of Pinot, half the hummus, half the baba ghanouj (flatus be damned), and a substantial portion of the chicken. A stick of jasmine incense filled the air with the smell of scorched flowers. She had turned all the lights on because harsh light is the enemy of the erotic, and she wanted all those dirty pictures of Rich fully visible and impossible to deny. Besides, now that she was drunk and the food was cold, what was the goddamn point?

"What's all this?" Rich asked, dropping his briefcase by the door. He looked around as if he'd never seen a kitchen. He made a face: "What's that smell?" Then: "What's that on the dining room table?"

"Food," Grace said. "And incense." She tried to smile and found she couldn't. "And on the table... just get yourself some food and sit down. It'll all make sense in a minute."

Rich fanned the air. "You call that incense? It smells like dog vomit. You were robbed."

"I picked up some Lebanese food," Grace said. "Since you're leaving for another trip to Europe and I won't see you for a while, I thought we'd have a nice dinner together. Maybe talk some things over."

When Rich gave her another of his tight smiles, and his eyes hardened at the corners, Grace swallowed a sob.

Just get through this, Grace. Remember, you've got the upper hand. If you can manage not to give it away.

"That's really thoughtful of you, Grace. Thanks. I haven't eaten yet, and it smells great."

Grace couldn't believe he'd even acknowledged her efforts. She pushed the words *dog vomit* out of her head and in a state of near-shock, hurried to fix him a plate of food. When she apologized for having to microwave it, though, Gloria appeared for a mental bitch-slap. *Why are YOU apologizing to HIM? He was supposed to be home two hours ago! And do I need to remind you what's all over your table?* Grace ignored her mother and, when the food was ready, served it to Rich, who was leaning against the kitchen island.

While Rich devoured his food, Grace slipped out of the kitchen to put on the music she'd picked out. Most days she considered their entertainment system entirely too complicated, just another piece of stage dressing for the aggressively affluent. Now that she knew how to direct music to the discreet speakers mounted in the kitchen, she appreciated the investment. Sometimes it paid off to let boys have their toys... as long as the toys didn't have a pulse and wear makeup.

"Good wine," Rich said through a mouthful of food. A crumb of chicken slipped out the corner of his mouth, and he absently wiped it away with the back of his hand. "What is it?"

Gloria asked, *He can't read the label?*

"It's a Pinot Noir from Oregon," Grace said. "Jigsaw. I'd never heard of the winery but I liked the label. It had one of those little cards with a review from the people at the store. It's good, isn't it?"

Oh shit, honey, you're slurring.

"But how can you trust the people at the store? Maybe they post those comments to sell bad wine," Rich said. "They can't say *this is dog piss* so they write *lively oak and citrus notes, and a long finish – highly recommended!* Then people buy it by the case."

"Don't they have a reputation to protect?"

Sit down, Grace, before you fall down. You're hammered.

She dragged a stool over to the island and sat far enough from Rich to keep him from smelling her breath.

To change the subject, she asked the time of his flight. Anything but the real focus of her interest, the pictures. Which he seemed to be ignoring.

"Fucking 6.00 AM," Rich said. He swallowed the bite of chicken in his mouth, then washed it down with a gulp of wine. He didn't wipe his lips before drinking. Grace fixed her attention on the oily smear he left on the rim of the glass.

Men, Gloria said.

Grace couldn't help but agree.

"Six?" she asked.

Rich nodded. His face looked like a thunderstorm about to break. "Fucking idiot travel agent we use. Air France and United both have non-stop flights to Paris but we're on fucking American through fucking Miami."

Grace started to say something conciliatory about Miami, but thought twice. She couldn't actually think of anything nice to say about the Miami airport, and her Mexican diarrhea quests had ruined him on travel.

"What time are you being picked up?"

"Limo's coming at 3.45," he said.

"You make it sound like a death sentence."

"The limo's coming at 3.45, Grace. That means I have to pack, get some sleep, and get out of bed before three. It's not just a death sentence, it's cruel and unusual."

"You can sleep on the plane, can't you? I mean, they're putting you in business class, aren't they? Or first?"

"First," Rich said.

This is the longest conversation we've had in six months. The thought struck Grace like a meteorite. It flattened buildings and left a blast zone the size of a small city. Emotional Hiroshima.

"Make love to me," Grace said.

Rich's hand stopped in midair. From the look on his face, Grace might have just asked him to spear his own throat with his fork, without eating his bite of chicken first.

"Make love to me, Rich," Grace said. The tears came and she couldn't stop them. "We haven't... in... I don't know... please, Rich."

"Tell me about the pictures first."

"The pictures?" Grace's mouth dropped open. "Oh. Them. Dammit, just go look at them..."

"I already know what they are."

She crumpled. She put her face in her hands and sobbed.

"Grace, your detective was good but *you* weren't exactly discreet. I've known all along. What is there to talk about, now that it's out in the open?"

"I... just..."

"What, Grace?"

"Make love to me." She held her head down. She couldn't meet his gaze. "Please, Rich. I want to go back to the way we were. Make love to me, please…"

Somewhere in the back of her mind, she felt Gloria hovering. Her mother radiated contempt and disgust. Crying like this. Begging her husband for sex, when it should have been the other way around. Grace shoved her intrusive bitch of a mother into the darkest corner of her mind and continued crying, trying not to make much noise, trying to keep from making a spectacle of herself. She already knew Rich found her revolting. Bawling would only make it worse, but she couldn't stop the tears. She tried; her face hurt from the effort.

She forced a state of calm upon herself, at least long enough to pour another glass of wine and toss the contents down her throat.

"Please, Rich," she said in the tiniest voice she could produce.

When he said "all right," she didn't believe him for a minute.

She stared at him as if he had just spoken a foreign language.

"All right," he said.

What was this little sideways smile on his face? She hadn't seen it before. But it didn't matter, did it?

"All right, Grace," he said. "If that's what you want."

She didn't believe this was happening. There was enough Pinot left in the bottle for another glass. She knocked that back, too, then followed him into the bedroom.

CHAPTER FOURTEEN:

ROBERT

A late-night phone call. Dehydration and disbelief. Film.

Robert's cell phone disrupted a stroll down a Quartier Latin street in Paris, with James. They had finished a meal and going to get an aperitif at a *pa-tisserie* around the corner... in the distance, Robert heard tinny strains of *La Marseillaise*. Nothing seemed out of the ordinary. The canned melody persisted. Robert thought longingly of Pernod, experienced a moment of dislocation (*oh wait, I'm really hearing that*), and opened his eyes. At first he didn't know where he was. The bed smelled familiar and unfamiliar at the same time. Freshly laundered flannel sheets, a nice touch in this clammy summer weather. What the hell time was it, anyway? That sense of being unstuck in time disappeared when his memory banks warmed up: the conversation, the trepidation, and Robert's utter disbelief when James had crawled across the sofa and kissed him earlier that evening. Exhausted from the ordeal with Grace and the long drive back, Robert's first thought had been *I just hallucinated that*. Only he hadn't.

"I love you," Robert blurted, after his heart crawled back out of his throat and he could talk again. He sat on the end of the sofa as far from James as he could push himself, expecting shrapnel to fly. The armrest dug into his lower back. He couldn't look James in the eye. "I'm crazy about you. You know that, don't you?"

James said nothing. Robert looked up and saw him shaking his head. He hadn't screamed yet, so that was a good sign, and none of the objects on the coffee table would make a good weapon. Hope unfurled.

How could you not know? You didn't want to know, Robert thought. *Just try denying that. Not that I'm going to ask.* He held his tongue and tried to suppress this twinge of irritation. No point being uncivil to someone you're trying to talk into loving you back.

"I've been dumped twice in a row," James said. This time, he wouldn't meet Robert's gaze, but he didn't move away when Robert slid closer to him and took his hand; nor did he look disturbed when Robert stroked his shoulder and upper arm. Blank, yes, but not disturbed, not revolted. "Sometimes I think there's something wrong with me. Stefan couldn't fix it. I think he tried, but he's not... he's not the answer to everything. We want him to be, and he lets us go on believing that, but it's not the truth."

"Maybe this is naïve of me," Robert said, "but what's wrong with you? I've known you a long time, and other than the fact that you didn't fall madly in love with me during law school, I can't find any flaws."

"I want too much, or I hope for too much too soon... I don't know. It must be something I'm doing wrong. The ones I want never want me back. Or they change their minds after they get to know me."

"I'd never dump you," Robert said. With splayed fingers, he combed James's thick hair. Had it been this lustrous before? This soft? "The doctor was hot but who needs a boyfriend too stupid to appreciate you? You're better off."

"It's not what you think," James said. "I really thought it would work both times. I always think it's going to work. Everything's fine, and I never see the end coming. Even when everyone else does. It's like the plane is coming in for a landing and all the other passengers have put their tray tables up and fastened their seatbelts, and I'm still standing in the aisle chatting with a flight attendant. But with David – the doctor – we went out how many times? It crashed before it got off the runway."

"At least you get to board the plane," Robert said. "It happens to us all. But we're here now, aren't we? I'd say we're in first class. It's nice, isn't it?"

James nodded absently.

He doesn't look convinced, Robert thought. And he could at least acknowledge what I said. He doesn't have to say he loves me back, but he could at least say something in the affirmative. That's not too much to ask for, is it?

He'd expected James to recoil at the subject of feelings, stammer apologies, and find an excuse to end the conversation. *I've got a long day tomorrow morning. It's a school night. That housing lawsuit. We're due in court at eight.* Some bullshit like that, but no, he hadn't done that. Nor had he made reference to several weeks ago – *This is just scientific. We're never going to do this again.* Science or no science, here they were, snug and warm in James's bed, naked. James was still fast asleep. Christ, he could sleep through World War Four. He looked peaceful, too, which he usually didn't, awake. And the phone wouldn't stop ringing. Robert resolved to change the ring tone; he'd had enough of *La Marseillaise.* Where had he left the phone, dammit? His jeans. The new ones he'd bought because the old ones fit about as well as two garbage bags taped together. Yes. He'd left his cell phone in the same pocket with his keys. Why the fuck was it still ringing? Why wasn't voice mail picking up? He looked back at James, who turned over and muttered something Spanish in his sleep.

Whoever's calling is hanging up before voice mail picks up, and calling back immediately. He knows what he's doing. I guess I'm more awake than I thought. At least one of us can sleep.

"Hello?"

"It's Rich."

"Rich? What time is it?"

"We're in the hospital. Grace had to go to the emergency room. I didn't know who else to call."

Robert's fuzzy romantic thoughts of James blinked off like lights.

"The hospital? Again?"

"*Again?*"

"Oh fuck. She didn't tell you? She passed out in a mud bath at the spa we went to. Had to be taken to the ER up in the Sierra this weekend. What the hell happened? Is she okay?"

"No," Rich said. "She's not okay. She's in the emergency room. Dehydration. Alcohol poisoning. They're talking about giving her a blood transfusion, for fuck's sake. I married Keith Richards. How soon can you come?"

"Alcohol poisoning?"

James stirred. "What is it?" he asked in a blurry, heavily accented voice. "What's going on?"

"Grace is sick. I need to go to the hospital," Robert said. *This can't be happening.* Then he spoke to Rich again: "Stanford?"

"Yes. Can you hurry? I never got to pack."

Robert's mind required an extra second to process this.

"Pack?"

"I'm leaving for Paris in three hours," Rich said.

"Your wife is in the hospital."

"I know. That's why I'm calling you, Robert. I have to go. You know that. We still work for the same law firm. You may not show up lately but you're still on the payroll. You know how things are. They can let you quote-unquote telecommute but they can't replace *me*. And she's not dying, you know. How soon can you get here?"

Robert wished James were awake enough to appreciate a wide-eyed *can you believe this shit* look. *I married Keith Richards?* But the lights were off and so was most of James's brain. Rich's too, from the sound of things.

"Yeah. Let me get dressed. I'm in the City. It'll take about 45 minutes."

He's still going to Paris. Motherfucker.

James mumbled, "Is Grace all right?"

"Apparently not. I have to go, okay?" Robert leaned down to kiss James's forehead. Another wave of disbelief washed over him. Rich was going to Paris, and leaving Grace in the hospital. After all this. "I'll talk to you in the morning."

*

Two hospitals in two days, and for the same reason: Grace thought she could starve herself into shape. Somebody should have told her that the body requires food. Just because you're overweight, you can't simply stop eating. You won't deflate.

Well, there was one option: Stefan. Whether Grace liked it or not, she was going to see him as soon as he had an opening. If necessary, Robert would carry her to Stefan's apartment on a stretcher, push her there in a wheelchair, or drag her by the hair. He refused to stand by and watch her kill herself like this. Especially not for her prick of a husband; he'd ceased to be a credible excuse months ago. This wasn't high school, where she could decide to eat nothing but white food for a few days until she puked up a mess of sugar, leeks, and Wonder Bread. Robert wanted her to grow up and move on. Or at least begin taking better care of herself.

Robert's arrival felt like the changing of the guard. Nobody smiled. Rich looked tired and annoyed but not concerned enough for Robert's liking.

Your wife is in the hospital, you douche. You could at least pretend you care.

Could Rich tell what Robert was thinking? Robert had his doubts but didn't care. The reason he'd been so obsessed with Rich all this time now eluded him. His looks? Easily replicated. Stefan only needed a photo. It would be like picking out a hairstyle from the magazines in the barber's lobby, or a design from the wall of a tattoo shop. Rich's skill as an attorney? Rich made a better impression – he cut a better figure – but absent the personal, just going on the strength of the work, Robert could eat him for lunch and spit out the bones. Charisma? Maybe. If he were a straight woman he'd get wet around Rich, but the man was too much of a backslapper for Robert's comfort. What was the appeal, then? The Lancia? The bulge in the front of his trousers? The envy of knowing Rich would make partner and Robert wouldn't, because law firms are really no different from fraternities or even cliques in junior high? Below the surface, everything's a popularity contest. From Robert's new vantage point, none of this made sense.

"Have a safe flight," Robert said. He crossed his fingers behind his back and wondered how much insurance Grace had on him.

*

Grace lay in her ER bed, looking even sicker now than yesterday. The docs decided against a transfusion, and were giving her fluids intravenously.

"We'll have a room for you in about an hour, okay?" The nurse on duty offered them a motherly smile, although she couldn't be out of her mid-thirties, their own age. "If there's anything you need, you let me know, okay?"

"Morphine," Grace croaked. "Or heroin, if you have some. Maybe crush a couple of Oxycontin tabs and mix them in."

The nurse's smile fractured at the corners. She stepped away from Grace's bed.

"I'm sure cocaine suppositories will do if you're out of opiates," Robert offered. "She looks like she could use a pick-me-up. Don't you think so?"

"I'll just bring you some ginger ale. How about that?"

Grace nodded once.

"What the fuck happened?" With Rich gone and the nurse out of earshot, Robert could no longer restrain himself. "Grace, what the hell did you do? Alcohol poisoning? Didn't we just go over all that yesterday afternoon, when they released you?"

Grace looked like an eighty-year-old grandmother who has seen war and famine, has buried a few of her children, doesn't understand why she has survived this long, and hopes it'll all be over soon.

"I don't know," she said. "Nerves, I guess. I'm a wreck. It seems to be my new resting state."

"And alcohol poisoning was supposed to calm you down? Being rushed to the ER in the middle of the night is soothing? Next time I think I want a Valium, I'll do this instead. It'll make me feel so much better."

"Rich is going to Paris in the morning. He left me here," Grace said. Robert could barely hear her. She stared up at the ceiling, and her vacant look frightened him. Stefan. As soon as possible, she had to see Stefan. "Can you believe it? I'm in the hospital and he just left me here."

"Maybe he knew you were going to be okay?" Robert's disdain for Rich could have withered a cactus. "I mean, if you were dying…"

"He'd have called his insurance agent to make sure the policy was up-to-date," Grace said.

"So are you going to tell me what happened?"

"I was nervous," Grace said. "No, I wasn't nervous, I was fucking terrified. Everything was riding on this. It was supposed to be perfect. It *was* perfect. Except for the part about me being terrified and fucking everything up."

"What did you do, Grace?"

"I used the photos. I spread them all out on the table, and when he got home…" She stopped for a minute, and looked down. She clenched the flimsy hospital blanket, kneaded it. "I wanted it to be a seduction but it wasn't. That's what I told you, and everybody else, but I was putting down an ultimatum at the same time. I put everything on the line. What if something went wrong? What if… you know, what if he didn't want me?" Her eyes shone but the tears didn't fall. She kept staring up at the ceiling. Robert leaned over and tried to make eye contact, but she didn't respond. Everything about her said *I give up.* "This was it. Nothing up my sleeve. *He knew about the photos, Robert. He knew all along. And he didn't care.* All it boils down to is, he didn't want me."

"What do you mean? Fuck! How did he know?"

Grace shook her head. "He said I gave it away somehow. I have no idea. He wouldn't say. And I was so drunk, even if he did tell me, it's gone now. I can't remember a goddamn thing. I'd been drinking all afternoon because I was a nervous wreck. I didn't think about dehydration. It never crossed my mind at all. The wine was just supposed to be a sedative. In addition to the pictures, I had all the food ready, the flowers, the music, and then he was so late getting home… by then, what was I going to do? I kept right on drinking, told him about the photos, and it didn't work." She crumpled again for a minute, not sobbing but chewing on her lip. Her face twitched in raw agony. "Next thing you know I just threw myself at him."

Robert had no idea what to say to that.

"It was awful, Robert." Her voice broke. "I'm so ashamed. You have no idea."

Actually, he did, but this wasn't the moment to say so.

"I can't believe I fucked things up so badly," she went on.

"You didn't fuck things up," Robert said. He took her hand. "You have to believe me. Rich has done the abandoning here, not you. None of this is your fault."

"Except the ass that's the size of Jupiter? Isn't that my fault? He seems to think it is."

Robert shook his head. "Look at me, Grace."

She wouldn't.

Fine, then.

"Grace. It is not your fault. Do you hear me? *It is not your fault.*"

"I begged him, Robert. I begged him to make love to me. It all came down to that one thing. If it could just be like it was. Forget the pictures, forget the detective, forget the other women, just let us be Rich and Grace again, like before. We used to be so good together. And when he said yes, I didn't even believe him for a minute. How could he mean it? How could he be saying yes? I mean, look at me."

Robert thought about James. More or less the same thoughts ran through his own head several hours earlier. James had said yes, too, and Robert still struggled to believe it, but he could still smell James on himself, and could still taste him, so it must have happened. Otherwise, it was the best hallucination anyone ever had.

"So he said yes?" Robert asked, to get his mind off James. He needed to be present for Grace. Drifting back into the interstellar space between James's sheets wouldn't accomplish much right now. "Can you tell me what happened next?"

"Sure." Grace turned to glare at him. "It was bad enough that he kissed me like my breath stank, but I told myself it was just the alcohol. I'd had so much to drink. He stuck his tongue in my mouth but his lips were hard. He didn't want to be kissing me. It was so obvious. It wasn't my breath, either. It was me. He didn't want to kiss me, but it was like he had to. It was an obligation. That told me everything, but it got worse. I was already thinking *He doesn't mean it* and trying not to cry, but then I got sick. *Robert, I threw up when he climbed on top of me.* All over him, myself, the bed, everything. One minute I was just kind of sad, thinking how insincere he was, how it was supposed to be this beautiful moment..." She stopped talking. Robert held his breath. "It was supposed to bring us back together, and it didn't. I kept throwing up, and eventually I made it to the bathroom, and I passed out on the floor next to the commode. That's when he called 911."

"Oh my God." Robert squeezed Grace's hand.

"It's over, isn't it?" She looked up at him in horror. "I thought I had a chance until tonight, but I think it's really over."

"I think that's up to you," Robert said. "What does your heart tell you to do?"

Grace shut her eyes again and seemed to sink into the thin emergency room mattress.

"My heart tells me to send that detective to Paris," Grace said. "And my head tells me to make sure he has plenty of film."

"Sounds like they're in agreement for once. That's an improvement. But Rich already knows about the detective and the pictures. Why bother now?"

Grace shrugged. "I've already bought the man a plane ticket. He seemed so happy..."

"That's no reason," Robert started to say.

Grace interrupted him: "I know it isn't. I'm curious, that's all. Curious and resigned to it. Now that the worst has already happened, what's left? What could he possibly do? Screw a French girl? What a surprise."

"Then why bother?" When Grace didn't answer, Robert continued: "If he does it after you've already confronted him, then you've got airtight grounds for divorce. As if you didn't have a good case to begin with."

"You can't ethically take the case – conflict of interest – but maybe you can refer me to someone who can?"

"You're not serious," Robert said. "You're going to do it?"

"Let's see what happens in Paris," Grace said. "And let's see how I feel when I've had some sleep. I don't want to commit myself to anything now. Not while I'm in this state. Right now, if it was up to me, I'd cut his goddamn throat, but maybe I'll feel differently later..."

"Right now you're too sick and exhausted to see things clearly. You'll get angry once you feel better. Then you'll be able to sort out your emotional state," Robert said. He wondered if this sounded preposterous. He doubted he had room to talk.

"Oh, I'm angry," Grace said. "And it's better that Rich is in Paris. I can only send the detective after him. If he were still here, I'd send thugs with chainsaws."

"You're beautiful when you're angry," Robert said.

Grace burped while saying "I know."

CHAPTER FIFTEEN:

GRACE

Diluted Nazis. Dreams of invisibility. Pallas Athena.

Grace was expecting the mysterious Stefan to look like a watered-down Nazi and he did. Not exactly blond, more of a redhead, and he had the high cheekbones and cool blue Siberian Husky eyes she associated with the animals on the stand at the Nuremburg Trials. At the same time, he had a nondescript air about him. She didn't feel repelled. Maybe it was the wrinkles at the corners of his eyes when he smiled, and the way his body language invited her into the room.

"Thank you for consenting to see me so early in the morning," she said.

"I wake up every day at 4.30," Stefan said. "I don't sleep much. I've never liked it."

Grace wanted to say something clever about the lack of baggage under his eyes but couldn't find the words. She could barely keep her own eyes open. Her brain felt like pasta boiled ten minutes too long. She didn't want sleep, she wanted a funeral: her own, with flowers and crying people and perhaps some Mozart in the background.

"You're not well," Stefan said.

"I noticed," Grace said.

Are you sure you want to take off your clothes in front of this man? Gloria seemed alarmed. *He may look like a Swedish porn star but honey, there's some-*

thing about him. Robert sees him how often? What do they do? It all sounds too sordid for words, and as a lady, you should not put yourself in predicaments like these. It's just not done.

Grace thought, *Well, I'm doing it. Nothing else has worked, and I don't know if you noticed, but I just got out of the hospital? For the second time in two days?*

"You're not alone with your thoughts," Stefan said. "You seem very pensive, but there is someone else in the room, yes?"

Grace snapped back to reality. "I'm sorry," she said. "Please forgive my manners. I'm completely exhausted. I'm drifting off into space. Did Robert tell you why I'm here?"

Stefan nodded. "Briefly, but I want to hear it from you. In your own words."

"Look at me," Grace said.

"I am looking. I want you to tell me what I'm looking at," Stefan said.

"I'm a mess." Grace welled up again. The black tides of depression flowed in, creating whirlpools and a strong undertow. She was drowning. "My husband…" She couldn't finish the sentence.

"Don't tell me about your husband. He's not here. Or if you think it's important, tell me later. For now, I want to hear about you."

"Look at me," Grace repeated. "I'm overweight. I've tried everything and I can't reach my ideal weight, and I'm sore all the time because it's getting to be such a strain on my body. The doctor says I shouldn't get pregnant. Surgery scares the hell out of me or I'd have done it already. But I'm afraid of my future, if this keeps up. I'm afraid of what I'm going to look like. I'll have trouble walking. I'll have a hard time finding clothes that fit. And the worst thing is, I feel like I've done something wrong, failed somehow, and it's driven Rich away…"

With this, she broke down. The last few hours – days – weeks –

crashed into her. One minute she felt morose but still functional, and then the grief knocked her down and pinned her helpless. She could do nothing but cry. When she tried to hold back the tears, her face ached from the effort. This had happened to her too many times lately. She gave in, and let her misery run its course.

"Let it out, Grace," Stefan said. "There's nothing to be ashamed of. You've been through a lot. Let it out."

"*I'm in hell*," Grace sobbed. "Oh my God, I'm in hell."

She fumbled in her purse for a tissue, couldn't find one, and for a minute was too flummoxed to continue crying. How could there be no tissues in her purse? She'd just bought one of those little travel-sized packages of Kleenex, and put it in her purse not even a week ago. Of *course* she had tissues in her purse... and as she thought these things, her frustration collided with her grief, enhanced it, exaggerated it... and she was crying again... *here comes the flood.*

"I think you might like a cup of tea, perhaps?"

She'd momentarily forgotten about Stefan. Only thin people can carry off that degree of unobtrusiveness. Robert dreamt of invisibility – she'd seen him press himself against walls all their lives, trying to merge with the paint or the paper – but Stefan actually succeeded. She could almost see through him, to the dated Nagel lithograph on the opposite wall.

"A cup of tea would be lovely," Grace collected herself enough to say.

She alternated between annoyance at the flotsam and jetsam in her purse – where did all this shit *come* from? – and sheer despair. She remembered her last reconnaissance mission before the Paris trip: trying to center herself by loitering at her car, thinking she might be completely empty inside, wondering if her future would be one long corridor of slamming doors. Where had all the time gone? Where had her goddamn *husband* gone?

"Earl Grey?"

"Anything you have," Grace called. She'd have said yes to a cup of gall and wormwood, or sewage, or tar. She dabbed at the corners of her eyes and told herself this would be over soon enough.

*

"We should begin," Stefan said. "When you're finished with your tea, I'll step out of the room. I want you to undress completely, lie on your back, and drape your body with this sheet. If you have any concerns about your modesty, I promise you I will be very discreet."

Meaning he'll say it was an accident, Gloria said. *When he's up to the elbow in your twat, don't say I didn't warn you, honey.*

Grace sipped tea. She wondered how it had cooled so quickly without him diluting it. For a man who can pull the pounds off with his bare hands, though, cups of tea couldn't be much of a challenge. She thought he needed decent china, but from the look of his apartment, he also needed a live-in maid and perhaps a flamethrower.

When she finished, she followed Stefan into the adjoining room and took a tentative seat in the armchair he gestured to. She wondered if she'd have to pee halfway through the... procedure? What should she call this? Massage? Bodywork? Supernatural corpulence mitigation? She couldn't find the words and decided to quit while she was ahead.

Stefan left the room.

Here goes nothing, Grace thought.

She carefully stepped out of her clothes, holding onto the edge of what she guessed was a massage table for support. Her head wouldn't stop spinning. She tried not to look at her own body. Even though the room was empty, she covered her breasts with her arm. Climbing up onto the table took a bit of effort — why wasn't it lower? — and when she covered her body with the white sheet Stefan had indicated, she thought, *This is the stupidest thing I've ever done.*

Gloria agreed with her. *Why don't you hang a sign around your neck that says RAPE ME? Have you lost your mind? You're never going to be seen again. I'm convinced of it. The police are going to dredge little pieces of your body out of the Bay in a couple of weeks, and don't say I didn't warn you!*

Grace said, *At least if I'm dead, I won't be around to hear you gloat. How do you say "I told you so" in Spanish? Is Juan tired of hearing it yet?*

Stefan returned.

"You seem distracted," he said. "There seems to be a presence in your thoughts. It's important that we are the only people in the room. Can we do that?"

"We can try," Grace said.

"I have an idea," Stefan said. "Normally I like for people to talk to me more, before I get started, but I think today I will make an exception. The talk is only a formality. Once I've begun, I always find out what I am dealing with. So, Grace, would you like to take a little nap?"

"I'm not sleepy," Grace said.

"You will be," Stefan said.

And she was.

*

"Grace, wake up. You've been asleep a long time."

Someone had replaced her tongue with a skein of wet yarn.

"It's time to wake up," Stefan said.

She recognized his voice now, his accent. God, how long had she been out?

185

"Don't sit up yet," he cautioned, when she tried to move. "Give your body a few minutes to adjust to the changes."

"Changes?" It took effort to get the word out. A deliberate concentration of will. This felt like the aftermath of an ugly visit to the dentist, when her mouth was still packed with cotton and the drugs hadn't worn off yet.

"Yes, I got a lot done today. It was quite surprising. Your body is very easy to work with."

"Am I thin now?"

Stefan chuckled.

Grace looked around now, feeling less disoriented with each passing second. Who chose this weird avocado color for his walls? These pictures? Nothing made sense, least of all his taste in décor.

"I managed to purge your system of several things it didn't need. Including some weight, yes. More than I usually take off during the first session. You'll notice a difference."

She wanted to leap off his table and inspect her body in the nearest mirror but her limbs wouldn't budge. In her sleep he must have filled her torso with concrete.

"I'm going to let you lie here for a few minutes, and I'm going to step outside. While I'm gone, I want you to lie still and relax. There's no hurry. Will you do that? Lie still and give yourself time to wake up more completely?"

"I guess," Grace said.

"That's good. I'll be back soon. Take deep breaths, relax, and enjoy this moment of quiet time."

Grace idly wondered if he'd left her breasts the same size. To come out of this flat-chested would be appalling, wouldn't it?

Her careful journey down from Stefan's table felt like climbing out of a car she'd wrapped around a tree. She expected pain but felt... well, nothing.

186

Did this mean she was in shock? She felt like a passenger in her own body. And when she put on her clothes – bracing herself on the side of the table to step into her panties – a shockwave hit her: they were *loose*. In a burst of optimism, she'd worn track pants with a drawstring, a pullover top, and a light jacket against cold San Francisco breezes.

Mary Shelley must have had this experience sometime in her life, to have come up with the idea for Frankenstein's monster. I should ask Stefan how old he is and where he's really from.

Grace stopped herself. Did she really want that question answered?

Any minute now Gloria would chime in with some unwanted burst of insight, but she seemed to be keeping to herself for the moment. Grace welcomed the change of pace. Blessed silence. When she finished dressing and Stefan still had not appeared, she decided not to keep waiting. She opened the door and stepped into the living room and...

"We were wondering when you were going to finish up in there," Gloria said. "I was just telling Stefan you take forever in the bathroom, and this is really no different, when you think about it."

Grace looked from her mother – her three-dimensional, tangible, un-questionably *there* mother – to Stefan, and back.

"I pulled her out of your mind," Stefan said. "I wouldn't have been able to get any work done, otherwise. I've never seen anything quite like it. Well, no, there was one time in Stuttgart..."

Gloria had on a robe that clearly belonged to Stefan. It was a mascu-line dark blue, quite heavy. She didn't seem to be wearing anything else underneath, not that Grace wanted to see for herself.

Grace took a heavy step backward, and then another.

"One minute I was in Havana with Juan, and suddenly I was here! Just like that! Poof!" Gloria exclaimed, waving her hands. "It was like pulling a rabbit out of a hat, only I was the rabbit!"

"Poof," Grace said.

She sat down hard and leaned against the door, which swung open behind her. The world went dim for a few minutes.

"Poof," she said again, and passed out.

*

Back home, in a familiar environment, the surrealism subsided. Grace lent Gloria some clothes – items bought out of the naïve or optimistic intention of "slimming into" them – and they almost fit.

"Let's go get some things in my sizes," Gloria said. "This dress looks all right. If anybody asks, we'll tell them I was backpacking in India and still have Delhi belly. That'll scare 'em off, won't it?"

Grace could only imagine.

"Now that Juan knows where I am," Gloria continued, "There's no need for me to rush right back, is there?"

"I guess not," Grace said.

She directed her mother to the same guest bedroom Flora Trust had just occupied ("Why don't we both freshen up a bit before we go out?"), then raced to her own bathroom to inspect herself. Had Robert gone through this? How had he not gone nuts? She felt *different*. The skin on her face felt taut, and – not to put too fine a point on it – she wasn't waddling when she walked.

Grace stripped and spun in front of the mirror. She still saw a fat girl but not as much of one as she'd seen yesterday. Between the pill-enhanced starvation of last week and whatever Stefan had done, she calculated a loss of about 30 pounds.

What did Stefan do with the bloody red Jello he scooped out of fat ladies' thighs? Did he have an incinerator? Did he eat it? Grace didn't want to know.

"*I feel pretty,*" she hummed. "*Oh so pretty…*"

She tried a pirouette but lost her balance. Okay, so she was still too ungainly for ballet moves. That would take a few more visits.

The big thing was, she'd lost weight! She had done it. It had happened. It was real.

It can't be…

But it is.

She turned her back to the mirror and looked over her shoulder.

That ass is smaller than it was last week. It's smaller than it was this morning. Stefan's got his work cut out for him, but what the hell, if he made Robert look like an underwear model, he can turn me into Claudia Schiffer.

*

Grace offered to bribe Stefan into clearing space in his schedule for at least three more sessions.

"Oh, I have plenty of money, don't worry about that," he said. "Don't even give it a second thought. I'm always happy when the clients are happy."

"There's a bottom line," said Grace. "And it's not just about your happiness with my bottom."

"You're right, there is, but don't worry yourself. I'm free Wednesday morning and Thursday morning at 11.00, if that's not too early?"

"Three in the morning wouldn't be too early. I'll be there."

"And bring your charming mother along. I've never gotten the chance to chat with someone I conjured out of a client's thoughts. Did you know you had that strong a psychic link?"

"I'd never given it much thought," Grace lied.

"I'll do a little cosmetic work while she's in town. No charge at all. I want to explore how I was able to bring her here. There must be something about her own physical make-up... but I won't get technical on you. Please bring her along."

"I don't think she'll mind at all."

Grace thought about Gloria at the boutiques in Palo Alto, Gloria at the salon getting her hair done. Gloria drinking three or four glasses of green tea per day. *White tea's higher in anti-oxidants, and even rooibos tea has amazing properties. You can't drink enough of this stuff! It's the elixir of life! Why do you think Asian people look so youthful well into middle age?* At least this time the voice was real and not emanating from the folds of Grace's cerebral cortex.

Mike called Grace on her cell phone Thursday afternoon, interrupting a walk along the San Francisco Bay waterfront. Grace liked parking in one of the airport hotel lots and strolling along the shore, staring across the bay. The sun sparkled on the water. Planes took off and landed. Here was a Lufthansa jetliner coming in from... where? Robert would know. Frankfurt? Munich? That sounded right. Grace didn't think you could fly to Berlin nonstop from San Francisco, but she usually let travel agents worry about details like that. If she wanted to fly down to Los Angeles or back East, she didn't mind buying tickets online, but for the big overseas trips, she wanted to talk to someone who knew more than she did. A couple of Alaska Airlines jets took off, one right after the other. A United flight, one of the big wide-body jets, came in for a landing, looking like it would crash into the water instead of landing on the runway that jutted out into the Bay. Grace hated that about the local airports: on arrival, she always worried about drowning.

"It's Mike," said a staticky voice.

Gloria nodded and watched the planes.

Jet-engine roar drowned out what Mike said next.

Grace screamed *I can't hear you please repeat that*, and Mike tried again.

"I'm in Paris, back at my hotel," he said. "Thanks for sending me here. I want to say that first. It's really… thanks."

"I'm glad you're enjoying yourself," she said. "Is everything all right? Is there a problem? Have you been able to find Rich?"

Gloria shot her a look. Amazing, what a couple of hours with Stefan could do. Her mother looked more like a sister now than Flora Trust did. The crows-feet at the corners of the eyes? Gone, erased. The liver spots on the hands? No more. And Grace couldn't be sure, but was her mother's bosom fuller? The hips a bit slimmer? Very probably so.

Grace herself, having now shed almost 50 pounds, felt as if she could leap into the air and land on the wings of one of these jets. She hadn't felt so light since college, and at the time she hadn't been paying attention to such things. Major shopping excursions seemed to be called for, but at the same time, why overspend now when she'd be thinner next week?

On the other hand, why not?

"I found Rich, all right," Mike said.

"Good, good. So has he been up to what we think he's been up to?"

"There's really nothing new to report," Mike said. Even with the staticky connection, even taking into account her mobile carrier's Propensity for Crappy Service, Mike sounded weary. "I can fax the pictures to your home, if you'd like. I've already had them developed."

"Sure," Grace said. "Is there anything I should know about them?"

"You're a nice lady," Mike said. "And you deserve better than this. You really do. I hope you're going to use these pictures for something… I hope you're going to help yourself, Grace. You can't keep on…"

"You're breaking up! I'm losing you! Hello? Hello?" Grace hung up the phone.

To her mother, she said, "He already knows my fax number."

"More pictures?" Gloria asked.

Grace nodded.

Another plane took off, British Airways this time. London. Grace wished she were on it. She wished she were someone else. Then she looked at her body again... did she really wish that? Well, no, not exactly. There's no reason to wish for something you already have.

"Let's go home," she said.

*

Half a dozen grainy pictures waited in the fax tray. Even dark, and with poor resolution, they told plenty.

"She's a whale!" Gloria said. "Oh my Lord, honey, I think she's even bigger than you were. Did you know they had fat ladies in France? I wonder where he found her. Maybe she's Russian or something. No, wait, they don't have food there, do they?"

Grace struggled to breathe. She looked at one picture after another, took a second look, and then a third, not believing.

Finally, she could speak: "He's toast."

CHAPTER SIXTEEN:

ROBERT

Vlad the Impaler. Dim sum. An ideal for living.

For a long time, Grace had been heading for a disaster. For just as long, Robert had known he'd be the one to pick up the pieces of Humpty Dumbass after her ultimate fall. Until now, he hadn't known what to use as glue.

He felt twinges of guilt, wallowing in hedonistic bedroom bliss while Grace courted disaster with Rich. Her seduction scene could never have worked: Rich was too far gone. Robert had always known Grace didn't have a hope in hell of winning him back, and Rich's reaction (or utter lack of one) to the detective's photos and Grace's collapse simply clinched it.

He wanted to shake some sense into his sister. He wanted to scream *THIS IS NOT THE WAY TO HAVE A NORMAL LIFE!* in her face. But then, what was normal about visiting Stefan?

Then there was James's smoking-pavement 180-degree change of heart.

He lay with his head on Robert's shoulder, and was nestled in the crook of his arm. Even in law school, their bodies hadn't fit together this well. (Robert weighed less now. Stefan had created more space to fit into.) They'd been sleeping together all week and as much as Robert loved it – every sweaty, straining second of it – doubts festered in the back of his mind: *Why is he doing this?* And, more disturbingly, *Why do I think he's miserable and trying to hide it? We look like a pair of fucking runway models.*

"What prompted you?" Robert had asked.

He shifted. His shoulder had grown sore, and James's leg shut off the circulation in his own leg, from mid-thigh down. Robert adjusted a couple of pillows – James liked to sleep with three or four extra ones in his bed, the big squashy kind meant for sofas. Black pillows, wine-red sheets, maybe a little on the brothel-overkill side, but he liked the colors and they set the right ambience for fucking. He didn't want to move if it could be avoided. It would require him to dislodge James and he didn't want to. Sooner or later he'd have to pee but for now, heaven on earth, bladder be damned.

"What prompted me to what?" James pulled the blankets over himself. They'd left the windows part the way open, and a chilly breeze blew into the room. The air smelled like two flavors of salt: the Pacific, and their exertions. "What, did you mean why did I pull up the sheets just now? I'm cold. You got me all sweaty."

"You know. Me. This." Robert looked into the glossy depths of James's hair, smelled sweat and shampoo, kissed him on the ear.

That's odd. Robert noticed a couple of tiny hairs growing in James's ear canal. Not the kind of detail Stefan would overlook. *But do I mention it?* He decided not to, for now.

"I'm bummed," James said. "I'm not getting out the sack-cloth and ashes over him, though. How long was it? Measurable in weeks? I'm bummed, not suicidal."

"But me, though," Robert asked. "Before, you weren't interested. How did this happen?"

He knew he shouldn't ask. He wanted to shut off the outside world and spend the rest of forever lying in bed with James, smelling his hair and talking with him like this. He wanted to tongue James's nipples and his armpits and the back of his neck. He wanted to lick a wet trail down the length of James's spine and blow a slow cool breath across his back, to make him shiver. Some quality of the light – late afternoon sun filtering through half-closed blinds – filled Robert with pangs of vague sadness. He considered the evanescence of their situation. Pale blue walls; deep blue mood. James didn't know what he was doing. Robert saw it clearly and wished he couldn't. He swallowed the lump in his throat but another formed in its place.

"I don't know. Something's different now. We're different," James said.

He looked away but continued stroking Robert's abdomen.

"We have visible abdominal muscles," Robert said. "That's what's different."

"For both of us. I'm different in other ways, too."

"I noticed." Robert could still feel the difference James was alluding to, when he shifted. Some of Vlad the Impaler's victims had smiled on their spikes. "Believe me, I noticed."

"There's something you're not saying. It's that you think I didn't want you before, because of your weight. Is that it?"

"No use denying it," Robert said. They'd known each other too long for bullshit, and they were both lawyers.

"I can't say it's not a factor," James said.

"So if I weren't thin now, this wouldn't have happened?"

James pulled away, then rolled over and looked at him. *Stefan is an artist*, Robert thought. *He understands subtlety. Even if he overlooks an ear hair or two.*

Or had he really overlooked them?

No matter. Had James ever been this handsome? How had Stefan taken away the preliminary unraveling of age – the wrinkles at the corners of his eyes, the sprinkling of white hairs, the vertical crease on each side of his mouth – without eradicating that tortured edge that gave James so much appeal?

"You're putting words in my mouth, Robert."

"Maybe you're looking for consolation after the doctor dumped you? Maybe I'm some kind of rebound? I've always been Grace's teddy bear; why shouldn't I be yours too? It seems to be my role in life. No matter what I look like."

"That was low. Why not just say I thought you were disgusting until you lost weight?"

"Didn't you?"

One more visit to Stefan, and then I'll be perfect. Monday morning, Robert climbed the stairs to Stefan's apartment. The thought distracted him: he stopped replaying the conversation with James and contemplated perfection. He'd already asked Stefan to remove every mole (except two, for character), every blemish, every ounce of unnecessary fat. Stefan had reconstructed Robert's face: a discreet nose job, a delicate facelift. The narrower nose, the absence of those sag-lines where his ears joined the sides of his head… all steps down the road to perfection. Putting his clothes on felt like a crime.

And he kept having to buy new ones as his body changed.

"You're asking for an exemption from time," Stefan said after the previous session.

Robert shrugged. He stood up carefully, feeling glorious in his own naked skin. He had never felt this comfortable, this powerful.

"Why not? If it's possible? You've exempted yourself, haven't you?"

Stefan nodded. "I have."

Today, Robert wanted Stefan to search deep. *Find anything that might be a tumor in the making. Anything that looks like it might fail – kidneys, liver, pancreas, lungs. Anything. How are my Islets of Langerhans holding up? How long is my hair going to last? Don't let it fall out again; I don't want to be bald. What about my teeth? Do I have ulcers? Anything that looks like it's going downhill, put a stop to it.*

Stefan had replied, *Stop the clock, you mean.*

Yes. Then break it.

But today the first thing Stefan said, on welcoming Robert inside and offering him a seat, was, "Let's talk about the cost."

Robert swallowed the rock in his throat and said, "Let's." He filmed with sweat. His heart pounded. He took a seat on one end of Stefan's battered leather sofa, close enough to the armrest for comfort, half-expecting Stefan to say *You can keep your body but what I'm really interested in is your soul. May I have it? It's not too much to ask for, do you think? It'll make a great snack, with some crackers and beer.*

"I have given you a perfect body," Stefan began.

Robert stared at the stack of magazines on Stefan's coffee table: *Stern, Conde Nast Traveler, Road & Track*… in other words, German bosoms, Santorini, and the new Porsche roadster. Next to the magazines, an overflowing ashtray leaked clove-scented ashes onto the dirty blue saucer beneath it. Robert recognized the curves of a fossilized bagel. Did Stefan smoke or did someone else? Robert couldn't decide whether smoking would revolt Stefan or whether he'd care at all. What's a little smoke to someone who can reach into the lungs and pluck out cancer cells like thumbtacks from a bulletin board?

"I was just thinking that while I was climbing the stairs."

Stefan nodded. "I know."

What could Robert say to that?

"So this does come at a cost. Grace and I have already discussed our terms, actually. This morning she called and made me an offer I couldn't refuse. She took me by surprise, and that doesn't happen often. A remarkable woman, your sister. Your mother, too. I'm very intrigued by your family. What must your father have been like? He figures prominently in your sister's thoughts. It's almost an obsession."

"He had a heart attack. She found the body. She's never been the same since." Robert looked down at the coffee table again. He hated this subject. "I guess you've already figured that out for yourself."

Stefan looked at him for an uncomfortably long moment, then nodded.

If Grace had been fragile and a little unsteady before their father's death, she certainly hadn't benefited from it. He'd always wondered how rushing into the bathroom after hearing him cry out and fall down in the shower had affected her, whether it was the reason she was so desperate for a quiet suburban life where nothing ever happened, and so desperate to be someone she wasn't. Someone who had never been hospitalized for a couple of days after seeing her father in the bathtub naked and dead, with his eyes glazed over and hot water cascading down upon him. She wanted to turn back the clock for her own reasons. It wasn't just about her weight, and it wasn't just about Rich. She wanted to edit that scene out of her memory.

Robert told himself he had to stop thinking about this.

Maybe he should go to Santorini. Quit the law firm, talk James into leaving his nonprofit job, and hang out in Greece for a few months. There had to be a better way to live than the corporate Habitrail he'd boxed himself into. His diet of drudgery, caffeine, and exhaustion – he'd explode like a gerbil in a microwave if he had to spend one more day in law firm hell. Why was he always the last to pick up on these things?

"We were talking about the cost, right?" Robert prompted a change of subject.

"What means the most to you right now?"

Robert didn't know what to say. "My…" His what? He tried to think. His appearance? His income? His career? His cock? Talking about their father's death had derailed his, Robert's, train of thought.

"Your feelings for James, perhaps? You haven't been able to stop thinking about him," Stefan said. "Is that something you'd be willing to give up?"

"You'd take my feelings for him as payment? Or, like, I don't get to be with James but I do get to continue looking like this?"

"Something like that."

He did say he was only with me because of the way I look now. If that's all it's based on…

"Exactly," Stefan said. "He made it about your appearance and not who you are as a person."

How the fuck did he know that?

"No, but you do have to think about your priorities. So would you give James up for this? Would you relinquish him to go on looking perfect?"

"What, you want to go out with him?" Robert wasn't expecting this. He looked at the Nagel print on Stefan's wall. How old had Stefan been in the Eighties? How old was he now? 25? 100? 950? "I don't get it. We're not an item, we're just… I don't know what the hell we're doing. He's not mine to give."

"But if he were. Your feelings for him, are they a thing you could not live without?"

"I need to think about that."

"Why don't you think during the session? Time is a bit limited."

*

Robert felt a twinge of guilt afterward. He looked at his body in the mirror and liked seeing someone else looking back, someone who sort of resembled him but was much better-looking. Maybe he'd get something pierced, but what? Nipples, navel, nose? How about a tattoo or two? Rebellious ink to adorn this flawless skin Stefan had given him?

He thought: *What have I done to deserve this?*

Then: *Nothing, really. Right place, right time. It could have been anyone.*

"So what's the verdict?" Stefan asked.

He wiped sweat away from his brow and said it had been an intense session. Robert didn't want to know what that meant. As long as the result looked good and wouldn't be prone to the ravages of old age, he was content.

"The verdict? Shouldn't I be asking you that?"

"I didn't find anything you should worry about, if that's what you mean. You don't have cancer or diabetes. None of those terrible diseases. I've also completely reset your metabolism. From this point onward, it will be almost impossible for you to gain excess weight. Your appetite will be minimal. You'll want only enough food to sustain yourself, but you won't be prone to bingeing and nibbling and craving junk food. You'll never have another blood sugar crash."

Robert surveyed his body: the flatness of his abdomen, the ridges of muscle. He looked like a sculpture, yes, but now he was more Michelangelo's David than Reclining Buddha.

James, though. Robert couldn't get the doubts out of his mind. He squelched one troubling thought – *Did I really put words in his mouth?* – and flexed his muscles. James had never spared him a second look until the pounds melted away. Sure, they'd ended up in bed together before, but that was cold manipulation borne from mutual misery. Robert didn't know how else to get close to James again, and had resorted to borderline coercion.

I'm a horrible person, he thought. *But don't I deserve someone who wants to be with me for me? Not on account of my belly, or lack thereof?*

"Do you want to keep this body?" Stefan asked.

Robert knew that wasn't the real question.

When making a pact with the devil, had anyone other than Daniel Webster ever gotten the upper hand? Robert had his doubts.

"Yes," he said. "Absolutely."

Bring on the night, he thought. *Let's go to hell.*

*

Waiting for the streetcar, Robert called James's cell phone and got no answer. Where the hell was the train? Where the hell was James? Robert left a message and tried James's land line next. No luck there either.

A streetcar rumbled to a halt in front of Robert, and once he'd boarded, paid the fare, and found a seat (a comfortable distance from the obligatory muttering San Francisco bag lady and her radioactive death cloud of body odor), he called James's office.

"He didn't come in today," said Theresa, the receptionist.

"That's weird."

"That's really weird," Theresa said. "He usually calls. We've called him at home but he didn't pick up. Do you think he's sick?"

"Could be." Red flags unfurled and began flapping in the gale-force wind inside Robert's head.

Robert got off the N-Judah streetcar behind the Market Street Safeway, and walked around the corner to where the J-Church would emerge from its tunnel. Waiting for the next streetcar, his guts clenched. Stefan couldn't have done anything to James. The bit about giving James up, or giving up the possibility of a relationship? Even if there had been a catch,

201

Stefan couldn't do anything retroactively, could he? He may have a way with biology but he couldn't also have the ability to alter physics... that was the wrong science class.

"*Come on!*" Robert fidgeted.

After an agonizing five minutes, an outbound J-Church streetcar arrived. It lumbered uphill through Dolores Park, toward Noe Valley. James lived a block from the tracks, and often complained about the roar of the LRVs as they rumbled past, but today it was convenient. Robert knew something had happened, and felt culpable.

James didn't answer when Robert knocked. He had a key, and let himself in. It didn't take long to discover why James hadn't shown up for work this morning: he'd hanged himself from the ceiling fan. For a minute Robert's brain refused to register what had happened. He shook his head in disbelief that James hadn't brought down the fan. *He's too heavy. That's not possible. He's not a big guy but he's not that light either. How is that possible?*

Reality caught up with him a split second later: HE'S DEAD, ASSHOLE.

His breath caught in his throat.

James hadn't undressed before ending his life. He delivered himself in his Sunday best, and the note pinned to his shirt shouted **IT'S TEMPORARY** in huge black letters legible from across the room.

"Oh Jesus," Robert whimpered.

The world faded to grey for a few minutes.

*

Robert got a knife from the kitchen and cut the rope around James's neck. The body crashed to the bed with enough force to knock Robert to the floor. He lay there a few minutes thinking about death.

I deserve everything that happens to me.

He unbuttoned James's starched white Oxford shirt. The prickly smell of dry-cleaning fluid wafted up from the fabric, along with hints of the organic thyme-scented deodorant James wore, and the smell of James's own skin. Robert blinked back tears. Or tried. They fell anyway.

I'm going to hell for this.

James didn't like undershirts – *hadn't liked* undershirts, oh Christ the horror of verb tenses when referring to the newly deceased – and wasn't wearing one now. Robert unbuttoned enough of the shirt to look at James's chest. The scar had returned: a livid terra-cotta goldfish.

IT'S TEMPORARY.

But was it retroactive?

James looked different in death. Worse? Robert couldn't put a finger on it. He had never spent much time with the dead.

"I'm going to hell for this."

Robert unfastened James's belt and unbuttoned his trousers.

"I'm going to hell for this."

It was temporary, all right. In death, the hair and fingernails of most corpses continue to grow. In death, James had lost a couple of inches and regained his foreskin.

"I'm going to hell."

Robert pulled up James's pants again and rearranged his clothes as best he could. He smoothed out all the wrinkles except for the ones in his own mind. Couldn't have the undertakers thinking he'd molested the corpse.

*

The police came. Seconds later, paramedics arrived to remove the body. Everyone was apologetic. So sorry you found your friend like this, are

203

you going to be okay, is there someone you can call. Robert answered questions, filled out forms. The police left with their paperwork; the EMTs left with James. The silent apartment was deafeningly loud. In a daze, he called James's office to break the news. The phone call to James's parents in Houston was the worst: tears, hysterics, gratitude, more tears. Terrible sobbing. Terrible guilt. *I did this*, Robert thought. *Stefan did this. I did this. I chose this. Oh my God. I'm going to hell.*

He wondered whether decapitation by a streetcar's steel wheels would hurt much. Would it be less painful to fling himself in front of a speeding BART train? Or at least faster? Dismemberment would be a hideous thing to survive. Limbs everywhere, blood, a mangled torso whose heart wouldn't stop beating. *No*, Robert thought. *I am not going to kill myself. If I do, it needs to be effective. If I'm giving up on my reason for living, it needs to be for an ideal death. I don't want to fuck up and survive. Stefan would just glue me back together afterward, and double his fee.*

I did this. Robert finally had something to think about other than his romantic obsession with James: accountability. Guilt. *I did this.*

But no, he hadn't done it. A couple of hours passed. He wandered around James's empty apartment, picking random objects up and turning them over. Books given as gifts. CDs and DVDs. The backpack he wore to work in lieu of carrying a briefcase. A broken glass in the garbage can. A toothbrush and razor forlorn in their coffee cup by the bathroom sink.

I did this.

But no. That didn't feel quite right.

Stefan had done it.

And Stefan could bring him back, too.

Robert raced out of James's apartment to hail a taxi.

He didn't expect to find Grace in Stefan's living room. Even less, he expected to find Rich sitting next to her.

"I made Rich an appointment with Stefan," Grace said with the sort of smile she had sometimes terrorized Robert with as a child. "Stefan's the most amazing massage therapist ever, and after the flight back from Paris, I knew it would be just the thing!"

"James killed himself this morning," Robert said.

Grace and Rich both froze with shock, Grace more convincingly than her husband. Robert could tell she meant it and he was faking to be polite.

"That's horrible," she said.

"I'm really sorry, man." Rich said, looking uncomfortable.

You don't know who James was, you fuckhole, Robert thought.

"That's sad news," Stefan said. "He was a kind man. He was a good client. I wish I could have done more for him."

"For him?" Robert asked. "Don't you mean, *to* him?"

"He stopped coming to see me. I cautioned him against it, but he seemed to be struggling with some questions about right and wrong. *Ruptured psychological frameworks* is the phrase I have given that predicament." Stefan turned his attention away from Robert for a moment. "Rich, would you like to come inside? I can tell you are quite tired from your flight."

They left Grace and Robert alone. Robert wanted to shout accusations in every direction but didn't know what else to say. He suspected Stefan would not respond well to being blamed. Besides, what was the crime? Time travel? Breaking the laws of physics to commit retroactive murder?

*

205

"He's undressing now," Stefan said, emerging.

"I hope you'll enjoy this as much as I will," Grace said. "You're satisfied with our arrangements?"

"More than." Stefan smiled and bowed slightly.

"You killed James," Robert said.

"James killed himself." Stefan's smile never wavered.

"What's that bullshit about *ruptured psychological frameworks?*"

"As I told you: it's a little something I came up with to describe the effect of enhancing beauty and subsequently taking it away," Stefan said. "May I suggest you leave now? I have a lot to do."

"What do you want?" Robert asked in a quiet voice. The implications were sinking in. "Underneath it all. What the hell do you really want?"

"I like lining up the dominoes, to watch them fall," Stefan said. "That's all. I've lived a long time and I've seen everything. I simply want to keep myself entertained. You and Grace ought to go eat something, I think. I'll be spending a few hours with Rich. In fact, I believe I'll spend the rest of the day with him." He winked at Grace. "You won't recognize him when I'm done."

Grace blushed.

"I don't see what you're objecting to," she told Robert. "Look at it this way: you'll make partner."

"How could you?" Robert asked, still silent and overwhelmed.

Grace looked him in the eye. "Don't pretend you blame me, Robert. And don't pretend you care about him. I did, desperately, until he went and fucked a woman the size of a brontosaurus in France, just to spite me. While I was in the hospital. I tried to get him back and he made me ridiculous. The fucking prick deserves everything he gets."

"And what is he going to get?"

"What he deserves," Grace said.

"Who *are* you? Who have you turned into?"

"You could ask yourself the same question. Who do you see when you look in the mirror? I don't know and I bet you don't either." Grace's voice could have chipped ice. "You really want to know who I am, Robert? Dad beat the crap out of me when he caught me having sex with David Boyer," Grace said. "Remember him? The boy from two doors down? Cute, freckles, auburn hair?"

"Dad always did have a temper," Robert interjected. "Not that it justifies anything. He beat the crap out of me often enough. Life calmed down a lot once he was six feet under."

"Dad threw David out of the house, and then he beat the bloody shit out of me," Grace said. "I didn't slip and fall in the bathroom when I found his body, Robert. He was kicking me. The doctors said I was lucky not to have internal bleeding, and they weren't sure I'd be able to have children. Afterward, he broke down and cried like a baby. He wouldn't stop apologizing. I told him to do the world a favor and go shoot himself, but I never thought he'd up and have heart failure half an hour later," she said, tearing up but looking disgusted with herself. "And I'm not sorry. He fucking deserved it. Don't say you never suspected." She looked at the door of Stefan's studio. "They both had it coming."

Robert felt himself being swept away by tidal forces. He couldn't control the outcome here. He felt full of helium – half his own already-diminished weight – as he bobbed down the stairs after Grace. Outside, he thought he heard screams emanating from the apartment above. Grace seemed oblivious, but then, she also seemed to be enjoying this.

She'd grown balls. Perhaps literally. Stefan was as immune to the limitations imposed by Mother Nature as he was immune to the ones imposed by Father Time.

Robert kind of admired Grace, now that he thought about it.

That sound couldn't have been screams, because Stefan had sound-proofed his apartment. Hadn't he? Maybe the screams were coming from somewhere else. Someone was watching a horror movie on TV in a nearby apartment. Or having kinky sex. In San Francisco, you never know.

IT'S TEMPORARY.

Words like wasps: did they only sting James, then, or everyone? James had stopped seeing Stefan, toward the end. Maybe Stefan held a grudge, and had undone the changes he'd made to James's body. Maybe something had happened between them. Robert couldn't get his mind around it. Did Grace know, or suspect? At this stage, did she still care? And Rich? What the hell was happening to him?

And did it matter?

"We should go to Yank Sing. I'm just dying for some dim sum," Grace said. "And if they don't bring out the *ha cao* fast enough I'll eat the wait-resses."

"How can you eat at a time like this?" Robert asked.

"Because I'm starving," she said.

And then the hunger hit him like a truck, like a meteorite, like a swarm of killer bees.

IT'S TEMPORARY.

But was it? Really?

All he could think of was devouring one portion after another of little Chinese dumplings. *Ha cao* and *siu mai* and *cha siu bao* and plates of steaming green *gai lan* spears and lots of jasmine tea and the plates themselves and the cups and the table and perhaps a couple of the wait staff, as Grace had suggested. Yes. Food. Best idea anyone ever had. When you've been exempted from the horrors of calories and time, why the hell not? And if your exemption expires, no one can say you didn't eat well.

"Dim sum sounds brilliant," Robert said. "Let's go."

Another scream came from the apartment upstairs, but the roar of an approaching streetcar drowned it out.

AUTHOR'S INDULGENCE

Thanks for advice, help, hospitality, moral support, and miscellaneous good deeds: JoAnna Ball, Dr Randal Beaton, Leng Boonwaat, Jerry Bu, Edward Cha, Jean-Daniel Chablais, Jessie Chabot and Rebekah Sheffield, Mitch Cullin, Juliet Do, Scott Erdman, Brad and Gina Gallaway, Raymond Hahn, Trebor Healey, Chad Helder and Tshombe Brown, Bryan Jones, Bob Kerr, Sang S. Kim, Woo-jin Kim, Justin Kowalczuk, T'jie Kwie, Noël Lebeaupin, Marc Lowe, Jason Luciano, Florian Meissl, Sean Meriwether, HyunSung Park, Jay Quinn, Christopher Rice, Rose Richard, Tammera Richards, Robert Rodi, Geoffrey Steinberg and John O'Brien, Joshua Susser, Jim Tushinski, Alexander White Tail Feather, Andrew Whittet, KK Wong, Joseph Wu, Dav and Mie Yaginuma, Jerome Yau, and Kristopher Yoon.

For editorial advice (among other things), I would like to thank Ellen Cotter, Douglas Ferguson, Jim Gladstone, Wil Hawk, and Andy Quan.

And I should offer a final word of appreciation to Jack Lee, Anthony Ly, and Daniel Warthling, who provided so much inspiration for this book. Truly, it wouldn't have been possible without them.

Marshall Moore
Hong Kong, January 2010